Bewitchery

TALES OF LOVE AND MAGIC

AMANDA SIRI HILL, RAE WILKINSON ,
REBECCA M ROBERTSON, INNA LYON,
WHITNEY OLIVER

Knotted Inkwell Press

Contents

Enchanted Stitches

Amanda Siri Hill

Meredith brought the skein of blue wool to her nose and inhaled deeply. The familiar smell of organic fibers mixed with the subtle scent of dye relaxed her anxious muscles. She hadn't realized how much she'd tensed up after teaching a dozen twelve-year-olds to knit. She knew it was important to pass on these skills to the younger generation, and she was committed to doing it, but she didn't know it would be so hard.

"Why is your hair so short?" one of the girls, Cassy, had asked as she showed her how to throw yarn over her needle. Meredith sported a pixie cut after buzzing her hair two months ago. She'd decided on a whim to get her hair permed, but instead of the lovely curls she'd hoped for, her hair had fallen out in clumps.

"I happen to like this look," she'd said, before forcing the conversation back to knitting.

Most of the girls were easy to work with, but this Cassy was a handful. From the moment she'd walked in, Meredith sensed a sharp edge to her.

A red, crocheted headband held back her raven hair which almost matched the color of her eyes. But it wasn't the dark eyes that put Meredith on edge. It was the pinch in her expression and the tightness of her shoulders.

"Why are you wearing a dress?" Cassy had asked while Meredith recounted the rhyme of the bunny jumping through the loop. "This isn't church."

Meredith had been especially proud of the outfit she'd put together and felt it complimented her short hairstyle. A flowy, floral skirt accentuating her waistline with a lavender blouse that hid imperfections in her figure.

Apparently tween girls didn't appreciate a well-put-together outfit when they saw it.

Meredith had struggled to keep her patience as the girls kept interrupting, especially Cassy. If they would pay attention, they would learn so much more. And faster. If they only knew that real magic hid just behind the basics. Once they could knit and purl, she could teach them how to use those stitches to their advantage. Combine them into hundreds of intricate patterns that when woven with intention would create scarves and beanies that did more than keep you warm on a cold, autumn night.

But she couldn't just tell them that. They had to take the first few steps on their own before they could be led to the real magic. Before they could knit from a grimoire.

Learning spells with yarn and needles required a balance of many parts. Instruction from an experienced witch, individual inspiration, and a pattern to follow. So far, the group of girls who had filled her yarn shop didn't seem to be the type who could figure out any of it. She would just have to keep teaching workshops until she found the girls she could help.

Cassy, on the other hand, could use a good silencing charm, and Meredith made a mental note to knit a teal ascot for her. The mix of green and blue, knit in complete silence, would calm Cassy enough to keep her from making rude comments. It wouldn't be strong enough to silence her completely—but she wouldn't want that anyway.

If Cassy had been an adult, Meredith would have cast a spell to ward her off the moment she saw her, but she was young yet and there was still hope. Generally, Meredith didn't allow anyone into her shop who might ruin the ambiance of magic and intention she'd worked so hard to cultivate.

Enchanted Stitches wasn't just a place to buy yarn—it was a place for anyone who needed magic. Tucked into the corner of a strip mall, it didn't look like much from the outside. But once inside the doors, bookshelves lined every inch of wall space, filled not only with books, but skeins of yarn in all varieties. Mostly wool as that was the easiest fiber to mold to your bidding, but also cotton for spells that required a little more stretch. Fragile fibers like angora were more limited as they tended to unravel if not bound tight with a hard-wearing workhorse like nylon. But nylon had its own problems with its unwavering rigidity.

The intricacy of blending the right fibers for the right job was not something young girls appreciated, or cared about. They were only interested in cute finished projects and didn't have the patience to understand the value of the time and energy channeled into each one.

And they especially didn't understand the magic that could flow from their fingertips as they wove sweaters, socks, and gloves.

Meredith had kept everything under control while the girls were in the shop, but now that they were gone, she could unwind with this perfect skein of superwash merino wool dyed to match the blue in her eyes. Not bright and arresting like most blue eyes, but dark and shifting—like a shadow.

She was about to drop into her favorite leather chair when she noticed a bracelet on the seat—the one Cassy had knit. She must have forgotten it. She hadn't done a terrible job, but there were a few twisted stitches. She stuffed it into her pocket, deciding to fix it later and get it back to her.

With a sigh of relief she relaxed into the chair and picked up her needles—only to be interrupted by the bell above the door chiming.

"We're closed," she said as she stood—her voice belying the patience she'd lost in the course of the evening. She'd forgotten to lock the door when the girls left.

"Sorry," said a deep, tentative voice with all the sincerity Meredith lacked.

It belonged to a man with hair as dark as Cassy's. He wore glasses and a confused expression, like he had no idea how he'd ended up in a yarn shop. From his high-quality jeans and collared shirt Meredith guessed he was more accustomed to the interior of an office, not an establishment of craft. He could probably throw out a spreadsheet faster than she could knit the ascot she had intended for his daughter.

Because this had to be Cassy's father. He had the same dark eyes, but instead of the edge and anger that filled the little girl's, his were arresting yet curious. The depth of his gaze froze her momentarily as she tried to find words. It wasn't just his eyes that intrigued her, but everything else about him. He was casually fit, only a few inches taller than she was, with hair that itched to go wild after a day at the office. When he smiled, one cheek curled slightly higher than the other.

He took in the hundreds of skeins of yarn surrounding him like they were part of a museum, his mouth hanging partially open. He kept his hands in his pockets, afraid to touch anything.

"Cassy forgot her headband."

His words broke her trance and Meredith found her voice, welcoming him to her shop. He looked barely old enough to have a twelve-year-old, which meant he had to be close to her age. There were hints of a story behind him. Like how he could be so polite and unassuming and be the father of such a brash little girl.

"I'm sure we can find it," Meredith said, leading him to the back where the classes were held. The room was a circle of mismatched chairs, some wooden, some wicker, some sofa-like, surrounding a coffee table that currently held empty soda cans, candy wrappers, and a mess of yarn.

It looked like it had been through a storm. A storm of children.

"It has to be here somewhere," Meredith said as she stuck her fingers down the creases of the brown leather chair Cassy had sat in. She didn't remember Cassy taking off the headband, but it was no surprise she'd missed something like that in the chaos of the class.

Something stabbed her finger and she jumped. It was a cable needle—sharper than a regular needle—and she hadn't realized she'd lost it.

"Are you okay?" Cassy's dad asked. "I didn't know you had weapons here."

She held up the offending needle. "It's just a cable..." She lost track of what she was saying when he smiled.

Wait. Was he flirting?

No one had flirted with Meredith in years, not if you didn't count Bart who came in every Tuesday hoping to get personal lessons she didn't want to give.

"I didn't catch your name," she said. "Are you Cassy's dad?"

"Jeremy," he said. "Thank you for teaching Cass, she really loves coming here."

He had to be lying, but his face looked genuine. More likely, his daughter was the liar, making him think she liked the class.

Meredith didn't try to hide her skepticism. "She does?"

"She pretends to hate everything," he said. "But if she stayed the whole time, she liked it."

She wouldn't put it past Cassy to walk out if she didn't like something, so maybe he was right. Maybe she'd misread the girl. She'd never been able to understand children.

Jeremy rifled through some of the mess on the table, half-heartedly checking for the lost headband.

"Did you ask her where she left it?" Why hadn't he sent Cassy in to find the headband herself? She would know where she took it off.

"She didn't say." He frowned. "We had an argument about it and I made her stay in the car."

At least she obeyed her dad.

Meredith checked the entire classroom and found nothing. Jeremy gave something of an effort, but hadn't been very helpful.

"Maybe I can keep an eye out and call you if anything shows up?"

He took a deep breath. "Actually this is a really important headband to Cassy. I can't tell you how difficult my life will be without it."

His words formed a pit in her stomach. That meant there was more to the headband than he realized. Meredith hadn't thought twice about it because there were millions of knitted items in the world, and only a few that held magic. She had no reason to believe the headband Cassy wore was any different.

"Why did she take it off if it was so important?" Meredith asked.

Jeremy looked as lost as any father of a daughter might be. Who knew why young girls did what they did?

"Where did she get it?" That was the most important question, and part of her didn't want to know the answer.

Cassy had been okay with her needles—for a beginner—but she didn't have the skill to make the headband she wore. Someone else had made it and given it to her.

"She brought it home from school one day saying it was a good luck charm from the lunch lady."

"Did she say the lunch lady's name?"

Jeremy narrowed his eyes as he thought. "Maybe Hattie or something?"

There weren't many witches who could weave spells with yarn, and it was a small enough community that everyone knew everyone else. If the woman who had given Cassy the headband was experienced enough to weave a proper spell into it, Meredith would have heard of her, or more likely, met her before.

"Do you mean Harper?" Even saying her name made Meredith cringe.

Jeremy didn't have to answer, she could see the recognition on his face. "That's it."

"We need to find that headband now," Meredith said. "Before it does more damage."

Meredith turned over every chair in the room, then swept everything off the table while Jeremy watched her with wide eyes, unsure how to help.

"Maybe I was a bit dramatic. It's just a headband. I can get it later."

No wonder she hadn't noticed any spells in Cassy's headband. Harper was terrible at knitting spells, which made them hard to detect. And Meredith hadn't been paying close attention. Who would have guessed that one of her students would show up with a piece crafted by Harper Owens? The chances were too high to be coincidental.

Harper had appeared in the witch community seemingly out of nowhere a few years ago, claiming she'd found a lost wool grimoire from an ancestor. A find like that was rare, and everyone talked about it for months. It was always exciting to have a new witch in the community, and even more exciting to have a new grimoire.

It wasn't unusual for a new witch to struggle with her weavings, and when Harper began to struggle, everyone was eager to step in and help, including Meredith. Her finished items didn't work like they were supposed to, taking unexpected dark turns. Instead of bestowing protection, a sweater would make the wearer accident-prone. Instead of enhancing the mind, a cap would cast a shadow of gloom.

There were so many ways a good spell could go wrong—something as simple as skipping a stitch in a pattern or using the wrong decrease. Woven spells were tricky and complicated to pull off. But no matter how much help Harper received, the problem persisted.

It took years for the truth to come out. Harper was never a part of the Owens family—she'd found an old grimoire, but it hadn't been handed down in her family. She'd stolen it from its true owner who'd gone missing.

What Harper never understood was that the heart of the spells, what really made them work, was the intention woven into the yarn. And she'd darkened every intention with her terrible deed. There was no way to salvage her work.

When Meredith ignored Jeremy's last comment, he spoke again. "Cassy will be fine. It's not a big deal."

"How long has she had that headband?" Meredith didn't look at him as she asked, too busy checking under the shelves of yarn in case it had fallen underneath.

"I can't remember." A hint of distress crept into his words.

Good, Meredith thought. He needs to be worried.

"A month or two, I guess." He pulled yarn from the shelves, making more of a mess than helping.

"Does Cassy's mom know more?" Dads didn't usually keep track of details like that, but the mother would know. "Can I call her?"

He took a moment to answer. "Cassy and I haven't seen her mom since she left years ago."

Meredith paused for a moment and glanced at him. That was a story for another time. A missing mother and a darkly magic headband explained a lot about Cassy's behavior and Meredith felt terrible for the unkind thoughts she'd had about her. She should have been more patient.

"Can you get Cassy from the car?"

As if sensing a desire for her presence, Cassy arrived. The bell over the door dinged.

"Cassy," Meredith said as she stood from her search on the floor, rushing to the little girl's side. She tried not to sound out of breath or worried, but from the look on Cassy's face, she'd failed.

Meredith could already see a difference in the girl's complexion. Her anger had softened to fear, and her edges had curved into innocence. If she'd been wearing the headband as much as her father implied, it had been affecting her mood and her personality for a long time.

Many of Harper's incompetent spells were nothing worse than bad luck, but she'd imbued a few items with truly evil spells. Their existence was legendary, but Meredith and the community had destroyed them. Or at least, they thought they had.

"Cassy, sweetie," Meredith said again, this time much calmer than before. "Where did you get that headband?"

Cassy looked to her dad for permission to answer. Good girl.

Jeremy nodded. But instead of answering, a look of fear crossed the little girl's face.

"She said I'm not supposed to talk about it," Cassy said.

"Cassy," Jeremy interrupted, frustration creeping into his voice. "What have I said about keeping secrets? Meredith is here to help."

Cassy's eyes welled with tears and Meredith looked to Jeremy, slightly shaking her head. They had to be careful not to scare her. He meant well, but it wasn't helping. She wouldn't talk if she was afraid.

He nodded and pulled Cassy close. "I'm sorry sweetie, I'm not mad," he said. "I'm just worried about you. Keeping secrets is dangerous and I want to make sure you're safe."

"But Mom..." Cassy didn't finish her sentence.

"Did you see your mom? Did she give you the headband?" Jeremy's eyes widened.

Cassy shook her head, but didn't elaborate.

Meredith jumped in to help. "Cassy, you are a talented and smart young woman. I could see it the moment you came in my door." That was true despite her snarky attitude. "Whoever gave you that headband isn't your friend."

Cassy, wrapped in her dad's arms, turned to look at Meredith. Her dark hair fell across her face, almost like a shield. They waited in silence for Cassy to answer, both of them giving her the space she needed.

His face was full of love for his daughter, which made him even more attractive. She had a hard time not noticing the crinkles around his lips and the lines of his jaw. Meredith knew her way around love weavings. If she were to make one for him it would be an oversized cashmere sweater in natural shades. Something light to contrast his dark eyes.

She made herself look away, she had to focus.

"The lunch lady gave it to me."

"What did she look like?" Meredith had to be sure, though she already knew the answer.

"She was old."

It had to be Harper.

"Do you know where you left the headband?" Meredith asked.

Cassy shook her head. "I don't remember taking it off."

"Could someone have taken it from you?" It would be worse if one of the other girls in the class had it now.

Cassy shook her head again.

Meredith ran her fingers through her hair and took a breath.

"It's probably best if you get Cassy home to rest," Meredith said. "Can I call you later?"

He looked as if he wanted to ask more questions, but after hesitating a moment, he nodded.

They exchanged numbers and Meredith tried to keep the heat from her cheeks as they did. He'd glanced at her and then looked away.

"Thank you," he said. "I've known for a long time something was wrong, but I had no idea what. I thought it was just puberty or something and I'm in way over my head with that. It's nice to know someone cares enough to help."

Meredith smiled, trying not to show the anxiety coursing through her veins. "Anything for a girl like Cassy."

He gave her a half smile before turning his attention back to his daughter.

"You go home and get some rest," she said. "And don't worry about the headband. Can I make you another? One that doesn't have to be a secret?"

Cassy nodded, but didn't look happy about it. There was something about that headband she wanted, and it had something to do with her mother. She'd only complied because her dad expected her to be nice, not because she cared about a headband Meredith could make for her.

If Meredith could be certain Cassy would return to her real self by not wearing the headband anymore, she wouldn't involve Jeremy or Cassy again. She would find the offending headband and take care of it herself. But if Cassy had been wearing it as long as Jeremy said she had, it would take some counterspells to lift the curse, and those could only be performed using the headband itself.

Until then she could make something to help Cassy through what would be a difficult separation. It would feel worse than the separation she'd gone through with her mother because of the strong emotions spells created.

She was glad to have an excuse to see them again, even though, for their sake, she wished she didn't have to. She walked Jeremy and Cassy to his white truck, bracing herself against the cold, January wind.

"Things are going to get worse before they get better," she said.

"You look cold," he said, taking off his jacket. She was about to protest, tell him she was just going to go back inside, but before she could, his jacket was around her shoulders. It smelled of oak and cinnamon and for a moment she forgot where she was.

"I don't know what's going on," he said, standing closer than he had before. "But it sounds like this is more than just a headband."

Meredith had never told a stranger she'd just met about her magic, and though she wouldn't do it now, she wanted to.

He didn't take his eyes off her as he waited, in silence, for an answer. Meredith couldn't find the words.

He shifted in the silence and when it became awkward, he said, "Thank you, again. For helping us. Call me when you find it, or when you know more."

Meredith nodded, wishing she could tell him everything would be okay. That she would make everything better and Cassy could go back to being the girl he knew before.

But she couldn't make promises she wasn't sure she could keep.

Meredith spent the entire night tearing apart Enchanted Stitches looking for the headband. At five in the morning she had to admit it wasn't anywhere in the shop. Though it was woven with magic, it still had to follow the rules of physics, meaning it couldn't just up and walk away on its own.

That left only a few options. The headband could have fallen off Cassy's head, but gotten wedged inside her shirt, or one of the other girls had taken it with them. Neither seemed likely. Harper would have woven an intention for the headband to stay on, and since it was crafted specifically for Cassy, none of the other girls would be drawn to it.

Meredith ran through her list of students, trying to guess who might have taken it. Truthfully, she didn't know enough about any of them to guess. She'd have to wait for a decent hour to call their parents and ask if any of them had come home with a cherry red headband.

Admitting defeat, she left for home, warm in the jacket Jeremy had left her. She needed sleep but that would have to wait.

The temperatures were starting to drop into freezing, freezing the ground enough she had to maneuver her Toyota Corolla carefully through the streets—a challenge much too difficult for her addled mind. Her apartment was in a new building in an old part of town where the city was trying to clean up its image. It meant she got a good deal for a nice apartment, and the only downside was the illicit drug deals going on in the parking lots across the street. Nothing she couldn't handle.

The inside of her third-story living quarters didn't look much different than the inside of her shop. Yarn and books filled every shelf and burst from the closets and corners, but the apartment had a kitchen and a bathroom with a shower, which the shop didn't have.

Even though she was exhausted, her mind wouldn't stop thinking about Jeremy and Cassy and the headband.

As she undressed to shower, she pulled from her pocket the small bracelet Cassy had knit. She'd forgotten about it. It felt like she'd put it there more than a week ago instead of a few hours. And instead of the annoyance that plagued her when she stuffed it in her pocket, she now only felt concern and sympathy for the girl.

As warm water spilled over the top of her head, it cleared her mind. She needed to find Harper and confront her, but not at the school. Kaylee, a fellow knitting witch friend, had a grimoire with a finding spell. A pair of gloves that could help the wearer find something they'd lost. She'd told Cassy she'd knit her a new headband, but she wondered if a pair of gloves would do the trick instead.

The clock on the wall read just past six in the morning. Plenty of time to knit a glove.

Once out of the shower she texted Kaylee, hoping she was a morning person and would respond quickly. By the time she'd dressed and dried her hair, Kaylee had sent the pattern.

Knit from Targhee wool in the same shade as the lost item, the gloves had a cable down the back and used lifted increases. Anyone else might have had trouble finding that specific yarn in their stash, but it was no trouble for Meredith. She was prepared for any wooly occasion.

Not all of her projects were imbued with spells and when she knit regular items she always turned on the television or listened to an audiobook. But when working a spell, distraction could break the magic.

She burrowed into her favorite spot on her couch in the living room, put Jeremy's jacket back on, and covered herself with a chunky blanket to begin the first glove. Throughout the process she focused on the stitches and the intention of finding lost things. As she worked, she wondered not only if the gloves would help find the missing headband but lead Cassy back to her mom as well. Though if Cassy's mom didn't want to be found, no amount of magic would bring her back—the gloves worked best on inanimate objects.

Meredith had to exercise strict control over her mind to keep herself from ruining the spell she was working. She wanted the headband to be found, and she wanted Cassy to find her mom, but a part of her—the part that didn't want to admit how she felt about Jeremy—secretly wanted Cassy's mom to stay out of the picture. It might complicate things.

To keep her thoughts centered, she forced them on Cassy.

The clock chimed eight before she knew it, and she'd already finished one glove. It was time to start the second, but she took a break to fix Cassy's bracelet. She didn't have a spell in mind for it, but she could feel the lingering aura of the annoyance she'd felt when she picked it up. It was time to fix that, and replace it with care and concern. It wasn't much, but it might help Cassy fight against the gloom in her life.

The task took longer than she expected, and she didn't have time to finish the second glove before she had to get back to open the shop. When she turned into the strip mall's parking lot, she was surprised to find Jeremy's truck waiting by the front door.

"You could have called," she said when she got out of her parked car, still wearing his jacket.

"It's not an emergency, and I didn't want to bug you, but I also don't know what to do. I can't focus on anything, so I came here."

"How is Cassy?"

He dropped his head. "Last night was rough. She slept, but she cried out in her sleep throughout the night. She called for her mom, she called for Harper, and she said a lot of things I didn't understand."

Meredith put a hand on his shoulder, wishing she could do more, but not wanting to be too forward. He leaned in and wrapped his arms around her, holding her like she was a lifeline to sanity. She put her arms around him and breathed in more of his scent, which was becoming familiar. She could get used to his strong arms around her, his hair brushing her cheek.

They held each other for a moment that got lost in time, and he didn't speak until she let go.

"I didn't sleep at all, and when morning came, I thought Cassy would be sick or want to stay home from school, but she didn't. She was more angry than usual, but when I tried to convince her to stay home, she yelled at me." He shook his head. "I didn't know what to do."

"It's okay," Meredith said. "I don't think anyone knows what to do." She paused, wondering how much to tell him. Whenever she chose to be honest about her profession people looked sideways at her and took a few steps back, never quite believing her. But Jeremy deserved to know, even if it meant he would slip out of her life. He hadn't even been in it that long, how could she be so sad about it?

"Harper put a spell on Cassy using the headband to hold it." It was so much more complicated than that, but it was a start. And too much would be overwhelming.

She pulled the half-finished gloves from her purse. "I made these for Cassy, sort of a counter spell. But don't get too excited, they can't reverse everything."

The bright red wool was like a beacon against the gray sky, brown leaves, and Jeremy's white truck. Looking at them, Meredith had to admit she'd done a fantastic job. They were so perfect they begged to be slipped on over her cold hands. What would she find if she wore them? Girls who wanted to learn witchcraft? A man who would stay by her side?

Jeremy took the one finished glove and ran his fingers over the fiber, adoring the beauty of the stitches. "You made this last night? After we left?" He hesitated before adding, "And it's magic?" Meredith nodded. "I made the gloves this morning, not last night. I searched for the headband for hours after you left." She gestured to her shop. "You can tell by the mess inside."

Through the doors they could see piles of books and yarn strewn haphazardly across the floor, empty shelves, and a cash register draped with roving wool.

"Let me help," Jeremy said. "I should have helped last night." His face brightened with the idea of a task to keep him busy. Something to help his daughter. "And you can tell me more about this magic."

"You want to hear about the magic?" He didn't sound like he was making fun of her, which would be a first. The few times she'd opened up in the past resulted in awkward stares and hurried excuses. She almost didn't believe he could be genuine.

He let out a breath. "I wouldn't have believed anything you just said a few months ago, but after what I've seen Cassy go through..."

She was grateful for his offer of help. In any other circumstance, she would decline, preferring to take care of her own shop, but this was important to him. And she was happy for an excuse to spend more time with him.

"Don't you have work or something?" she asked. It struck her how little she actually knew about the man in front of her. They hadn't had any of the usual get-to-know-you conversations.

"I took a sick day. I didn't think going to the office would be a good idea under the circumstances."

Smart decision. She didn't ask what he did for work, he'd probably tell her some corporate speak she wouldn't quite follow.

Inside the shop, Jeremy gasped. "It looks worse on the inside."

It was like a yarn rainbow had thrown up on the carpet.

Meredith let out a sigh. "Yeah. There's no way I'll get it back into shape before we open." She had regular customers who would show up as soon as the clock hit eleven and it would take a miracle to get things back to normal.

"Tell me what to do and I'll do it," Jeremy said. "And you can finish the gloves." He gestured to the project she held in her hands. He knew it was important, and even if it meant the shop wouldn't be ready in time, it was worth the sacrifice.

She never allowed anyone else to stock the shelves because she was particular about how everything should be put away, but how could she say no to the knockout who was eager to handle her yarn?

"Start with the superwash wool in the back." She pointed past the cash register to the classroom. "The shelves are labeled with the colors and you can match them up with the labels on the yarn."

He nodded and got to work, and so did she.

"You said you were going to knit her another headband," he called from the other room, "but you chose to knit gloves instead?"

Her practiced fingers moved so fast it was impossible to see what they were doing, but she didn't need to see the stitches to know they were perfect. "The gloves will help Cassy find the headband, and we need to find the headband to see what we are dealing with. We can't fix what we don't know is wrong."

"What if you wore the gloves?" he asked. "Would they lead you to the headband?"

She didn't dare tell him the truth. *No, they would either lead me to you if you're everything I think you are, or lead me away from you if you're not.*

"Doubtful," she said instead. "The headband belongs to Cassy and the gloves will only help the wearer find objects that rightfully belong to them. But don't distract me, I have to concentrate to make the gloves work." Getting sidetracked with feelings of desire would weaken the effect of the gloves.

Jeremy did as she asked and only interrupted her when he needed to know where to put something that wasn't labeled properly. He'd done a better job of stocking than she expected, but still not as good as she would have. As she cast off the stitches on the last glove, she fought the lack of sleep slowing her down.

"What time does Cassy have lunch?" Meredith asked. Harper would realize Cassy didn't have the headband when she saw her, and who knew what would happen after that.

"I'm not sure," Jeremy said. "Can't they give these colors names that make sense? Why is this purple called Dewberry? Is there even such a thing as a dewberry?"

The bell on the door interrupted them. Meredith had forgotten to lock it again. Too much on her mind.

"We're not—" She stopped when she saw Harper Owens standing in the doorway.

Cassy had called her old, but old was relative to a child. Harper was older than Meredith, but she wasn't ancient.

The wrinkles on her face were deeper than they should be for her age, and she'd let her hair grow out, an odd mix of sandy blonde and dull gray that looked dirty. Harper had stopped caring for her looks years ago, ready to embrace the wicked witch stereotype.

Meredith stood frozen, holding the finished gloves. No one had seen Harper for a long time. Everyone thought she'd escaped far away after her evil deeds came to light. She was never charged with the Owens murder she'd committed—due to some witchcraft on her part—but the entire witch community knew she'd done it. The law might not have been able to touch her, but if she'd stayed in the city, or anywhere nearby, the witches would have meted out their own justice.

Some had searched for months, never finding the smallest clue. And here she stood, as if she owned the place. Where had she hidden all this time? And why was she back?

"Harper," Meredith said. The word was more like a whisper, laced with accusation and fear. Meredith was stronger and more experienced than the woman who stood before her, but that didn't matter when Harper was willing to perform black magic.

She wanted to ask her when she'd come back, how she'd stayed under the radar, and how she'd gotten into the school. How she'd faked identification and background checks to find a job where she was constantly surrounded by children. But none of it mattered. She'd found a way, and Cassy was paying the price.

"Meredith." Harper's voice was laced with enmity, and a bit of a challenge.

Jeremy appeared from the back, took one look at the women staring at each other, and glared at Harper. Meredith could see in his face he understood who this was.

"What have you done with my daughter?"

She stepped between him and Harper. She wouldn't let him get hurt on her watch.

As despicable as Harper was, she had a hold on Cassy that had to be sorted out before they could dispense with her.

Harper gave them a knowing smile. She held all the cards.

"I heard my sweet Cassy came for lessons," she said.

Jeremy clenched his fists, his arms flexing. "She is not yours."

Meredith caught his gaze and shook her head. It would take more than physical strength to win this battle.

"What do you want, Harper?" Meredith asked, turning her gaze back to her adversary.

Harper smiled like they were all old friends. "I just want to help Cassy find her mom."

"Her mom left us," Jeremy said. "If she wanted to be found, we would have found her."

Harper's smile didn't fade. She'd picked Cassy because she was vulnerable and radiated her desires so intensely Harper could taste them.

Meredith didn't know what kind of woman Cassy's mom was, but as all children do, Cassy would blame herself for her mom leaving. She would think that if her mom came back, it would prove she was worth loving. Harper had taken advantage of that vulnerability.

"How generous," Meredith said. "You've moved on from murder to helping vulnerable children?"

"I am only here to help," Harper said. "There is nothing in it for me."

She didn't care about Cassy, or helping her find her mom, but she wasn't about to reveal her true intentions either. Harper could be doing this for a myriad of reasons, but if Meredith had to guess, the old woman was looking for the strength of youth. Whatever spells Harper was still trying to weave, they'd be fading with age. Certain spells needed a lot of strength, sometimes the work of multiple witches, and Harper was alone. She could only do so much.

"Did you send Cassy to my class?" It would be just like Harper to leave Meredith with the work of training a witch, then swoop in to steal her when she was ready.

Training witches wasn't easy, and worked best when they started young. Meredith tried teaching adults, but their stitching was always a little off, or the way they held their needles wasn't quite right. Habits that were nearly impossible to change once they were ingrained. She'd even tried teaching adults who'd never knit before, but they always ended up taking shortcuts that cut the magic short.

Harper had always looked for shortcuts, which was partly why her spells never worked. But instead of becoming disinterested in the work and forgetting about the magic one could weave with yarn, she'd turned to dark magic to compensate. She never understood you had to work with the intentions of the universe, not bend it to your will.

"She's quite talented, don't you think?" Harper said.

"If we find Cassy's mother," Meredith said, "you'll leave her alone?"

Harper's lip twitched. "Of course I will."

It was an easy promise to make. If Cassy's mom didn't want to be found, no spell would counteract her will, so no harm would be done. Harper wouldn't think twice about lying, but she had to know by now that if she broke a promise, it would weaken her magic.

"Release my daughter from whatever spell you put on her," Jeremy said.

Harper gave him a patronizing smile. "It doesn't work that way, son."

A vein pulsed in Jeremy's forehead when she called him son, but to his credit, he didn't punch her. Cassy was like Jeremy—strong willed and smart—which was exactly why Harper had chosen her.

"I gifted Cassy the headband to bring her out of her depression. You want that for your daughter, don't you?"

"It made everything worse. We just want it gone."

Harper shrunk a little. "Sometimes magic has a mind of its own."

The spell must not have worked like Harper intended it to.

Cassy wanted a way out of the emotional turmoil inside her, and it would be easy to believe a magic spell could fix it, but she'd have to deal with the abandonment at some point. Harper had only prolonged the inevitable, making it harder to face when it finally hit.

These were the things Harper never understood.

"If you truly cared about Cassy," Meredith said, "you'd release her from the spell."

Harper's lips drew into a thin line. "And let you steal her from me?"

Meredith had no intention of stealing anything, but it was exactly what Harper would do. And Harper couldn't understand anyone having good intentions when her intentions were only evil.

"You used a binding spell, didn't you?"

Harper's silence was all the answer she needed.

The headband drew Cassy to her, and Cassy had worn it so long that the original item wasn't necessary to keep the bind in place anymore. But to break it, they had to find the headband.

It was darker magic than Meredith had ever dealt with before. Magic that forced someone against their will. It always worked for a time, but blew up in ways you could never predict in the end.

"Where is Cassy now?" Jeremy asked.

"She's at school," Harper said, like there was nothing to worry about. She wouldn't do anything to make the police come after her. If Jeremy and Meredith went to the police with their story, they would sound crazy, and Harper knew it. She'd woven a tight web.

But she hadn't planned for everything.

Meredith picked up the gloves she had just finished.

Harper's attention was immediately drawn to the bright red cables and the expert stitching. As terrible as she was at her craft, she knew professional work when she saw it. A spell perfectly woven through the fibers of yarn, made with excellent craftsmanship and pure intention.

It was what Harper wanted but could never have.

"You can have these gloves," Meredith said. "If you release Cassy from your spell."

"I didn't put her under a spell." Harper could hardly look away from the gloves, greed filling her eyes. "Besides, we can't break it until we find the headband."

"I knit these for Cassy, hoping if she wore them, she would find the headband."

Harper sneered. "Unless her mom is the thing she wants to find the most. Then the gloves will be useless."

Meredith shrugged.

"I can take the gloves to Cassy and give them to her at lunch," Harper said.

"We don't need you to give her the gloves," Jeremy said.

Meredith held up her hand to stop Jeremy. She tried to communicate her plan through a look, but he was too upset with Harper to notice.

Meredith handed over the gloves, knowing Harper would use them for herself. It was a dangerous gamble, since Meredith didn't know what Harper really wanted. She wasn't sure Harper knew what she really wanted.

The tired, old woman inspected the gloves closely, paying attention to the stitching and the soft wool. "You aren't lying about the spell you cast, are you?"

Meredith shook her head. "That is only something you would do."

Harper sneered. "I don't need any self-righteous lectures."

"What about the headband?" Jeremy asked. He'd been quiet as long as he could.

Harper slipped the gloves on her hands, one by one, admiring the soft wool on her fingers. She stared at them a long time.

"My grandmother knit me a pair like this once." Harper's face softened and for a moment Meredith could see the lost little girl she must have been at one point. No one knew her past and what brought her to this point.

When she looked up from the gloves, her eyes focused on something in the distance. She pointed at the top of one of the shelves. "There it is," she said. "The headband."

It was in a place Meredith had checked no fewer than five times. It stood on the shelf, bright as a beacon, existing in a place it hadn't before. Even Jeremy's eyes widened as he turned to look at Meredith in surprise. Whatever she'd done with the gloves, they worked better than expected.

"Intention is everything," Meredith said to Jeremy. Not knowing what spells were intertwined with the headband, she couldn't say what made it disappear and then reappear again. But a working of sinister magic trapped in a shop full of sincerity must have wanted to disappear. Ashamed of what it was.

"I'll make you a deal," Meredith said. Not knowing how the headband was created, or what evil magic Harper wove into its depths, she would have a hard time figuring out how to counteract it. "Destroy the headband including whatever magic it holds, and you can keep the gloves."

Harper looked back and forth from Meredith to the gloves. The treasure she held—a strong working of magic that could instantly find lost items—was priceless and rare. She'd already seen how well they worked, and she would never have another opportunity to get her hands on so valuable an item. She certainly couldn't create something like that herself. But Cassy was a prize too. Meredith just hoped Harper was willing to cut her losses on the time spent grooming the little girl.

Harper ground her teeth. "I'll make the trade."

Jeremy and Meredith let out a sigh of relief, though Meredith knew she'd created a monster.

Harper stomped to the shelf with the headband and snatched it with a scowl.

"If the curse isn't properly broken, I rescind my gift of the gloves," Meredith said, making sure Harper couldn't cheat them. If the gloves were not properly gifted, they wouldn't work as well.

She scowled again before chanting something Meredith had never heard before. Knitting witchery didn't use chants—only patterns, fiber, skill, and intention. This was something different, and Meredith was glad she'd made the deal. She would never have figured it out. No wonder the headband had caused more trouble than any normal headband should have. It wasn't just an object with a poorly enacted spell—it was imbued with evil.

A shadow passed over the shop as Harper continued to chant, though there were no large clouds in the sky. Meredith's throat constricted and she gasped for air. Jeremy was having the same problem. He lunged for Harper, but stopped mid-air like he'd been frozen in place.

Meredith's arms felt like lead weights, but she didn't know what she would do to stop Harper even if she could. They needed the witch to break the spell and only then could they attack.

Jeremy was grimacing in pain.

Meredith's despair was as bleak, but for different reasons. She had knit the gloves Harper would use to find what she'd lost—power.

The spell on the headband was breaking, but once it was free, there was nothing they could do to stop Harper. Knitting magic was a slow art, not something she could pull out on a whim, and whatever Harper was doing had more power.

When Harper was done, she left with the gloves before either of them could move. Meredith thought when the witch left, her power to hold them captive would subside, but they continued to struggle for breath.

Something warm radiated from Meredith's pocket, distracting her from the oppressive weight growing around her.

Cassy's bracelet.

An object knit not by Harper, but by a girl under her spell. Traces of Harper's magic hid inside the bracelet, but Meredith hadn't been able to feel it before. That magic was then interwoven with Meredith's magic because she had fixed the bracelet.

It was difficult, but Meredith slipped the bracelet onto her wrist and air filled her lungs. She gasped and dropped to the floor, exhausted. As tired as she was, she couldn't take more time to recover. Jeremy still struggled next to her.

She reached out and slipped the bracelet onto his wrist. He collapsed on the floor next to her, and they lay side-by-side, hand-in-hand, catching their breath, the headband squashed between them.

Harper had meant to kill them. Meredith hadn't made any stipulations about that in the bargain.

"We have to find her," Jeremy said when he had enough air to speak.

"She knows how to disappear," Meredith said. "But she won't be a danger to Cassy anymore. We know to watch for her, and she's the type to work in the shadows where no one knows who she is or what she's doing."

Meredith picked up the headband, devoid of any evil magic. It was just a regular headband now, and Cassy could go back to being a regular little girl. But at what price? She stared at it for a few breaths, trying not to cry. Jeremy watched her in silence for a moment, then wrapped his arms around her, breaking any control she had.

His arms were warm and his shirt soft, and Meredith couldn't remember the last time someone held her close. It made her feel like whatever evil was out there, they could balance it out by something as simple as an embrace.

"I would say thank you, but I don't think it's enough," he said when her tears stopped and he let go.

"I'd love to see Cassy when she's up for it."

"As soon as I get up," he said, "I'm picking her up from school. You're welcome to join me."

"But the shop..." Meredith stopped. She owned the shop, she could close it for the day. "Let's go."

Jeremy stood up and held out his hand to help her from the floor. He put his arm around her waist and led her out to his truck.

"Just make sure to lock the door behind you," he said.

Keeping Horror in Order

RAE WILKINSON

A bit late for an espresso, don't you think?"

Ophelia jumped at the gravelly voice, but it was only Jack peering over her shoulder. She tried to laugh but managed a tired snort.

"I've got Hallow's Eve duty this year," she said, adding her specialty absinthe coffee creamer to her coffee and cradling her chipped Department of Creatures and Haunts (DOCAH for short) mug in her perpetually (and magically) moisturized hands.

"Ah, I don't envy you, my friend," Jack said. He itched absently at a tuft of fur behind his right ear.

"Wasn't the full moon last Thursday? Are you trying to keep some wolfishness going for your Hallow's Eve resolution?" Ophelia asked.

"Nah...it's always so crowded Halloween night–everyone starting their new projects all at once. I'll wait a few weeks for the enthusiasm to wear off before I start mine. It makes everything so much easier. I'm seeing a doctor next week for the leftover fur," he said, gesturing to his ear. "Lawrence says it's just a thyroid thing."

"Ah, well. Good luck with that," Ophelia said, heading for the door.

"No Hallow's Eve project for you this year, then? You're usually the first through the portal. You and your...lovely little friend," Jack called after her.

Ophelia paused, then turned to face him, arranging her face into what she hoped was beleaguered acceptance. "You know how it is. Everyone has to do their bit, don't they? I get the next three years off too, and Mariscaleth deserves the break so..."

Jack's smirk threw her off her ruse. He knew her too well.

"Right, right. It has nothing to do with a certain *someone*?" Jack's eyes sparkled.

"Of course not," she snapped, but her face was burning. "He doesn't even know who I am."

"Aha! I knew it. Don't sell yourself short, Ophelia Dreadwood. You're a force to be reckoned with. I'm sure he knows who *you* are." He waggled his eyebrows suggestively.

Ophelia felt on the verge of bursting into flames. Not literally, of course. She wasn't a phoenix. Any attempt to defend herself would only give fodder to Jack's teasing, so she huffed, spun on her heel, and rushed out the door.

"Good luck tonight!" Jack called after her sweetly.

Ophelia dropped into her chair at the portal access desk and sipped her coffee, trying to ignore the slight tremble of excited anxiety in her hands. She thought she had been discreet, but her crush—no, if she was being honest with herself, it was more of an obsession—had clearly been more obvious than she hoped. How humiliating. At least Jack wouldn't be here when Viktor Andrei passed through the portal tonight. He *would* pass through the portal tonight, wouldn't he? Ophelia's stomach tied into knots just thinking about it. It was the only reason she was here, no matter what she had tried to tell Jack.

For months she and Viktor Andrei had exchanged glances. She swore he always held her gaze a beat longer than necessary. Their longest conversation had been sixteen words. It had happened only a few weeks ago. He had slid into the elevator with her one day, just before the doors closed. Her whole body had erupted with prickling excitement.

"What floor?" she asked, gazing up at him through eyelashes that had conveniently just been enchanted to flutter long and thick around her bright green eyes.

"Thirteen, if you please," he said, his deep voice wrapping around her like a blanket. She pressed the button, fighting her shaking hands.

"The Archives," she said, feeling every atom of air between them. "Researching for your Hallow's Eve project?"

"I am." He leaned closer to her, and she caught a whiff of his intoxicating scent: pine with the slightest tang of something darker. She'd be lying if she said she hadn't tried for days to replicate it in the potions lab. Then, the doors had slid open at Ophelia's stop, and she regretfully left the elevator and the tantalizing smile of Viktor Andrei behind.

After the elevator incident, Viktor Andrei seemed to vanish. She thought she caught a glimpse of him leaving the agency one day, but by the time she rushed to catch up with him, he was gone. But tonight was All Hallow's Eve. He had been researching for a project, which meant he would most likely be exiting through the portal tonight–it was tradition for DOCAH employees to begin their horror distribution projects for the new year on All Hallow's Eve. Ophelia took a deep breath and settled as best she could in the lumpy office chair. The portal was open, the fluorescent lights above were buzzing, and her passage approval stamp was freshly inked. All she could do now was wait.

The first creatures to approach were the three Siren sisters. Ophelia carefully placed her earplugs in each ear and gave what she hoped was a professional smile to the startlingly beautiful women. Their dresses and hair dripped, but Ophelia noticed with relief that the water didn't reach the floor. She knew too well how often she would need the mop tonight, and she was grateful to be spared the trouble now.

"Passport and papers?"

The first sister's full-lipped smile revealed razor-sharp fangs. She handed Ophelia the midnight blue passport of Sea Monsters and a stack of approved project papers.

Ophelia knew she shouldn't have snooped, but her curiosity got the better of her, and she scanned the project papers before returning them. "A one-hundred-person sailing contest? How perfect!"

The three sisters smirked at one another and nodded at Ophelia as they passed. Once the last dripping skirt crossed through the purple haze of the portal, Ophelia removed her earplugs. The Sirens knew they were not to speak at the portal, but one could never be too careful. She imagined the chaos the sisters would inflict with the slightest envy, but the thought of missing her chance to see Viktor Andrei was enough to keep her in her seat.

A few hours later, Ophelia mopped up the mess of yet another putrid sea monster. "The night is only halfway over," she muttered to herself. "Plenty of time." She bumped into a creature that had been standing silently behind her and jumped so violently that she knocked over her mop bucket.

The old woman didn't apologize; she simply held forth her papers and passport. She held a large kennel in her other arm containing a writhing black mass of tails and mewling.

Ophelia tried not to stare at the woman's gray, decaying, cat-like face. She cleared her throat. "You're all set to pass through to Tianjin, ma'am."

The woman purred softly and stepped through the portal. Ophelia shuddered and sat again behind the desk. She picked up her worn copy of Dracula's memoir: *I Came, I Drank, I Conquered.*

She was so enthralled, she didn't notice Annabell until she cleared her throat.

"Oh, sorry, Anna!" Ophelia leaped to her feet. "Passport and papers?"

"No apologies necessary." Anna beamed, her jawbone peeking through the rotted flesh on her face. "I'm so excited." She handed Ophelia her Undead passport and slim project folder.

"The usual?" Ophelia asked, fighting a grin.

"You know they don't make sweets like theirs here!" Anna was practically vibrating with anticipation.

"What's your costume this year?"

Anna held up a white sheet with two holes cut out. "Ghost," she said. "Can you imagine their faces when I lift the sheet? The amount of candy they'll drop as they run away?" She giggled with delight, but Ophelia was only half-listening. She had just caught a glimpse of the clock. It was getting worryingly close to dawn. Disappointment coiled around her like a snake.

"Ophelia?"

"Right," Ophelia said, snapping her attention back to Annabell. "I think it's your best costume yet. And I know this is one of your favorite trick-or-treating neighborhoods."

"Yes!" Annabell said, clapping her hands. "Rich kids are the most satisfying to scare. They also pee their pants the most. Hey, wait a minute, what are you doing behind the desk?" Annabell asked, seeming to take Ophelia in for the first time. "Nobody pulls off Hallow's Eve scares like you! Aren't you trying for another award this year? Or are you finally giving the rest of us a chance?"

Ophelia fiddled with the pen on the desk, avoiding Annabell's gaze. "Oh, you know, everyone has to do their bit," she trailed off, the excuse she had given without hesitation to Jack sounding paltry in her ears, especially after the number of strange looks she had received through the night. Ophelia Dreadwood, winner of Most Horrifying Hallow's Eve Project for the last three years sitting at the *portal desk* on All Hallow's Eve? The rumor mill was sure to be running full tilt. She cleared her throat. "Promise to share some of your boon with me?" Ophelia asked, returning Annabell's papers to her eagerly outstretched hands.

Annabell paused for a heartbeat, staring at Ophelia suspiciously, then shrugged. "Always!" she called, skipping through the portal.

Ophelia sank back into her chair and dropped her forehead to the desktop. Viktor Andrei wasn't coming. He wasn't coming and she had wasted an entire Hallow's Eve on *desk duty*. She decided to wallow in self-pity until her shift ended. Hope was for fools. Love was dead.

Someone cleared their throat. Ophelia snapped her head up and promptly turned into an incoherent puddle. She gaped up at Viktor Andrei, drowning in the dark gold of his eyes.

"Aren't you supposed to ask me for my passport and papers?" Viktor Andrei asked with a flash of an easygoing smile, the light catching on his knife-edged canines.

Ophelia cleared her throat in a manner that was much squeakier than she hoped. *Get it together, Ophelia!* she chided herself.

"Right," she said, affecting what she hoped was a cool, calm, and collected tone. "Passport and papers?"

"I've got a special one this year," Viktor Andrei said, handing her his documents.

"Oh?" Ophelia's eyes flicked over the project. Windswept island. Minimal human settlement. Enchanted hare. Enchanted hare?

"A...bunny? Your project is to catch a bunny?" A smile tugged at her lips as she glanced up at Viktor Andrei's perfect face.

He laughed, a deep, rich sound that filled the room. "A *magical* bunny," he said, pointing to the page. "It hasn't been caught in two centuries, and it's said to bestow unbelievable power. That doesn't *tempt* you at all?"

Ophelia licked her lips, caught in his gaze. He had no idea.

"Anyway, I was hoping you'd want to join me."

She stared at him stupidly. "What?"

"Come now," he said, eyes dancing. "It's Hallow's Eve. You've been toiling away at this desk, probably cleaning all manner of unspeakable messes left by portal travelers, watching everyone else leave on their adventures. You deserve a break. The night is already over in nearly all of the time zones. How many more travelers could there possibly be?"

Ophelia bit her lip. She had hoped to see Viktor Andrei tonight, maybe even speak with him, but she never expected this. An invitation. Her legs felt like jelly.

"I don't know, Viktor Andrei." She relished the taste of his name on her tongue. "I'd be in deep trouble if someone noticed I'd left my post." She couldn't care less if someone noticed she'd left her post. She had a clean enough record that no one would bat an eye. But she couldn't seem too eager.

"Of course, of course," Viktor Andrei said with a sigh. He plucked Ophelia's empty mug from the desk and turned it so the logo faced her. "DOCAH," he said in a falsely authoritative voice, "Keeping Horror in Order." He smiled as he set the mug back down. "You're nothing if not dedicated, Ophelia. I only hoped to spend a little time with you...to get to know you better. Oh, and just call me Viktor. Viktor Andrei was my father."

Did he just say her name? He did know who she was. And did he say he wanted to spend time with her? Were all her Hallow's Eve wishes coming true? She craned her neck to look down the long corridor leading to the portal desk. It was deserted. Viktor was right, the time zone clocks on the opposite wall were nearly all showing times past dawn.

"Wait." Ophelia glanced at Viktor's papers again. "There's not much time until dawn on this island. Aren't you worried about..." She wondered how to delicately ask if he was worried about bursting into flames in the morning sun.

"Ophelia," Viktor said, leaning toward her with a roguish smile, "what is life without a little danger?"

Ophelia smiled back at him, excitement growing in her like a warm ember. A clandestine project, alone, with Viktor. Never in her wildest hopes did she imagine this happening tonight. "Oh, alright. It is quite rare for someone to show up later than this. No one will miss me, right?"

Viktor held out his hand. Ophelia held out his portal key. He chuckled, pocketing it and holding his hand out again. A blush crept up Ophelia's neck as she realized what he wanted. She took his hand. Despite the marble coolness of his skin, sparks danced up Ophelia's arm.

They walked through the portal together, and Ophelia shivered in the familiar caress of the swirling purple mist. A breath later, the mist was gone, as was the portal behind them.

Ophelia blinked, waiting for her eyes to adjust. The landscape before her slowly took form, lit by slanting moonlight. Tall silver trees surrounded them, their branches shuddering in the breeze high above. As they walked forward, still hand in hand, dead leaves crunched beneath their feet. The sea crashed against the rocks somewhere in the distance. Ophelia breathed in the night air, thick with the scent of decaying leaves and salty ocean spray.

"Is this place what you were researching in the archives?" Ophelia whispered. The forest seemed to demand reverence. It felt like a sanctuary, sheltered from the battering wind and waves beyond.

Viktor looked down at her, his eyes bright in the semi-darkness. "You remembered."

Ophelia flushed and looked away. Viktor gently brought his hand under her chin, turning her face back to his. He took in her expression as though trying to memorize it. Ophelia swallowed, willing herself not to swoon on the spot.

A twig snapped somewhere nearby, and Viktor dropped his hand. "Yes, this is what I was researching. This island has a remarkable history. You can feel it, can't you?"

Ophelia nodded. She was feeling a lot of things, being in his presence, but he was right; the air was practically humming with magic. The trees seemed to watch them as they passed, raising the hairs on the back of her neck.

"They say a secretive but powerful coven settled here hundreds of years ago. They lived for some time in peace, but when a sailor ran aground...well, that was the beginning of the end."

"It always is," Ophelia sighed, lifting her skirt to step over a rotting log.

Viktor flashed her a smile. "He wasn't a very bright fellow, and the witches scared him, even though they had nursed him back to health. He snuck off in the middle of the night and sailed back to the mainland.

"The witches thought they had seen the last of him. They were a little offended he had left with no thanks or farewell, but they carried on with life as it had been. The winter that year was rougher than they had seen, but their magic more than made up for bad weather, and their crops and animals flourished as they always had. On the mainland, however, things were dire. In our dear sailor's village, the animals were dying, the food stores were dwindling, and a plague was ravishing the old and the young alike. You know how humans get when they are hungry and desperate," Viktor said gravely. "They become more monstrous even than us."

"Too true," Ophelia said with a rueful smile.

"When the village turned on the sailor for bringing some sort of evil back with him from his journey, he was only too eager to turn on the witches who saved him."

Viktor paused, and Ophelia waited, hoping he would take her hand again.

Viktor took a deep breath, and in a low voice continued, "The villagers came, saw the prosperity of the witches, and burned every last one."

Ophelia shuddered, bile rising in her throat. She knew the story was likely just a legend the humans on the mainland told each other to keep them from attempting the treacherous journey to the island, but it wasn't exactly the romantic conversation she had been hoping for when she accepted Viktor's invitation. Surely he wouldn't enjoy rehashing tales of the Vampire massacres of 1514, so why did he think she would want to talk about this?

He slowed, scanning her face and frowning. "I'm sorry, have I upset you? It's only a tale. What would All Hallow's Eve be without a scary story?" He looked at her earnestly, and Ophelia managed a smile.

"Right, just a silly, scary story," she said, swallowing the bad taste in her mouth.

"Well, I don't know about silly, but anyway, the tale says that the last witch of the coven rained down lightning on the villagers before she was burned, taking more than half of them with her to the other side. A hare was struck by lightning, too, but instead of dying, it absorbed the witch's power. There have been many sightings of a lightning-quick silver hare on this island, but no one has managed to catch it. Yet." Viktor reached for her hand and squeezed it in excitement. Ophelia's worries and the sense of foreboding that had settled on her shoulders after Viktor's story fled at his touch.

Viktor's hand tensed in hers. He stopped, standing perfectly still, eyes darting at every sound. "Do you see that?" he asked, his voice barely above a whisper.

Ophelia squinted in the darkness, but nothing moved among the skeletal trees.

"Come!" Viktor whispered, and he pulled her deeper into the woods. Ophelia stumbled a little, but Viktor's grip kept her upright. The wind picked up, howling eerily through shivering leaves and branches.

Ophelia stopped abruptly. Viktor's hand slipped from hers and he hurried ahead, focused on something in the distance. How tedious that he kept dropping her hand, but her attention was caught by a strange melody she could just make out in the gale. Ophelia listened hard to the music. It was a nursery rhyme she vaguely remembered.

Ladybird, ladybird fly away home,
Your house is on fire and your children are gone,
All except one,
And her name is Ann,
And she hid under the baking pan.

As Ophelia listened, the melody grew louder. She whirled around, trying to find the source of the sound, but all she found were trees, trees, trees.

Ladybird, ladybird fly away home...
Ladybird, ladybird fly away home...

The singing grew louder and more dissonant. It seemed several, deeper voices joined the melody, becoming more insistent every moment.

Ladybird, ladybird fly away home...

FLY AWAY HOME
FLY AWAY HOME

Ophelia clapped her hands over her ears and squeezed her eyes shut, but the voices still filled her mind. Two strong hands landed on her shoulders. Her eyes flew open. Viktor stood before her, confusion and concern in his eyes.

"Ophelia," he said, giving her a little shake. "Are you alright, Ophelia?"

The forest was quiet, a gentle breeze caressing her cheek. Her heart pounded, blood rushing in her ears. Viktor looked entirely unaffected. Ophelia breathed deeply, her face flushed. What had just happened? Had the terrible singing truly all been in her head? This would be a terribly inconvenient time to succumb to madness.

She cleared her throat. "Yes, yes, I'm okay. I just...thought I heard something."

Viktor held her gaze for another beat, his mouth twisted and eyes narrowed. Ophelia took a step to the side, allowing Viktor's hands to fall from her shoulders. She didn't like the way he looked at her, like she was a deer, easily spooked, or a child in need of protection.

"Onward!" she cried, marching in front of Viktor. "Let's find your rabbit."

As they walked, she tried to keep up with Viktor's conversation, laughing weakly at his jokes and following him when he darted after every snapped branch and falling leaf. In reality, her ears were straining, wary of the return of the haunting melody. It was exhausting, and not at all how she hoped her adventure with Viktor Andrei, the man of her dreams, would go.

"Ophelia! Look!" Viktor said, snapping her focus back to him.

This time, she had seen it, too. A flash of white light, here one moment and gone the next. They rushed to the place where the light had vanished.

The light flashed again, just a bit deeper in the woods. Viktor raced ahead of Ophelia, disappearing into the shadowy trees.

Ophelia followed the sound of cracking twigs, but it faded far ahead of her. How was he running so fast? Needle sharp twigs caught at her dress and arms like grasping fingers.

When the woods ahead of her grew silent, Ophelia stopped, holding her side. She tried to take shallow breaths, listening hard. Nothing. Not even a breeze to stir the branches above. Her heart pounded. It was really very irritating. She was used to being the scarer, not the scared.

A whisper caressed her earlobe. *Fly away home...*

Ophelia whirled, but there was no one there. A crunch of leaves nearby, just beyond the light of the moon slicing through to the forest floor. She squinted in the direction of the sound. A figure: tall, broad shouldered, prowling, predatory.

"Little rabbit..." A deep, sing-song voice from the trees. Quite different from the nursery rhyme singers.

"V-Viktor?" Ophelia called, unsure.

A rumbling laugh was the only response.

Ah. This was an interesting turn of events. "Viktor," Ophelia said, adopting her "I mean business" tone usually reserved for unruly werewolves. "There's no rabbit, is there?"

"Of course there is," Viktor purred. "There's a rabbit every year, but I think this year's might be my favorite. You see, I've never had a rabbit show so much interest before Hallow's Eve as this one.

Especially not one so *formidable* on her own. Always glancing in my direction when she thinks I'm not looking. It's so...*delectable.*"

Viktor's crunching footsteps circled Ophelia, though he stayed out of sight. She wondered if he could see her furious blush. Viktor's stomach rumbling from the bushes told her he could. So stupid of her, to fall in love with a vampire, but what was she to do?

At least she wasn't utterly defenseless. Far from it, really. She reached inside her pocket for the silky black powder she kept precisely for moments like this, and threw it to the forest floor.

The leaves and branches covering the ground erupted in green flames and smoke, and Ophelia sprinted the opposite direction from the spot she had last seen Viktor's shadowy form.

Viktor's delighted laugh followed her. "Yes!" he cried. "Run, little rabbit!"

Ophelia rolled her eyes. Vampires could be so dramatic. She kept running, hoping a hiding place would present itself to her. Ophelia didn't wear seven good luck charms for nothing.

As she ran toward the sound of the sea, her mind wandered. It really was a clever trick, but how had Viktor pulled it off? The flash of light could have been something as simple as a concealed flashlight, spun into something mystical by the spooky witch tale and the general atmosphere of the island, but the singing was harder to figure out. Vampires didn't have magic, and the music had been much more invasive than what a speaker hidden in a bush could produce. She wondered–

Viktor Andrei dropped from a tree to block her path.

Ophelia skidded to a stop, leaning over to catch her breath. "How are you so fast?" she gasped.

Viktor grinned, the silvery moonlight glinting off his razor-sharp fangs. "My father was part Wendigo."

"Gross," Ophelia said, straightening.

"Not for my parents. They bonded over their love of human flesh. Brought them together even though they were different species. It's quite romantic."

"And there's no chance of us bonding instead of you eating me? Even though we're different species?"

Viktor took a step forward. Ophelia took a step backward.

"Bond over what, little rabbit?"

Ophelia stared back at him. She didn't know a blessed thing about him beyond knowing about his beautiful eyes and strong shoulders and muscular chest and...oh dear, she was getting carried away again.

Viktor took another step forward, licking his lips like she was an especially juicy pork chop.

"Uh, do you like coffee? Or, could we bond over...music?"

Viktor smiled. "I don't think that's going to work for me."

"Shame," Ophelia said, twirling her fingers in an intricate pattern behind her back. "I know some really great bands." Ophelia snapped her fingers, and shining golden ropes sprang out of thin air and coiled around Viktor's legs. He staggered forward and fell, releasing a roar of frustration.

"Get it?" Ophelia said as she was backing away. "Bands? Like, the binding kind?"

Viktor writhed on the ground, his eyes flashing.

"Right, so we're not going to *bond* over puns either, I see." Ophelia sprinted away again. She wasn't foolish enough to believe the ropes would hold Viktor forever, but it would at least buy her some time. Viktor had the key to open their return portal, but if she could just make it to sunrise, he would become a smoking pile of ash and the key would be hers for the taking.

She kept running toward the sound of the sea. Surely there were good caves for hiding, and at least she would be out of these horrible woods. The sea had certain other advantages as well, of course, but she hoped she wouldn't have to use them. It was supposed to be Mariscaleth's day off, after all.

After what seemed like ages, she finally broke through the treeline. She wasn't sure how much adrenaline could possibly be left in her system after the number of times she had jumped at Viktor-shaped shadows and trees. She took in her surroundings, heart pounding.

Moonlight slanted sideways over the remains of an ancient village. Moss and ivy clung to crumbling stone walls, bleached and smoothed by the wind and salty spray of the sea. Inside some of the ruined buildings were cauldrons so rusted, they would surely disintegrate with the slightest nudge. Even on the most weathered stone blocks, faint outlines of carved runes remained. Ophelia reached out to trace one, and a shiver swept up her spine.

Fly away home, something whispered in her ear. Her heart jumped into her throat, thinking of Viktor, but she was alone in the ruins.

So, there had been some truth to Viktor's story. A coven of witches must have lived here long ago, and they didn't anymore. And now they were warning her to leave. She glanced at the horizon beyond the village. The dark sky was smudged with lighter purple. Dawn was coming.

Ophelia placed her hand over a protection rune etched into a crumbling cottage entrance. "I'm sorry, my sisters," she whispered, imagining the horrors these old buildings had seen. "And thank you."

Ophelia found the center of the town, a small square with weeds and sea grasses poking up through the long-cracked stone. She crouched in the middle of the square and drew three runes in the thin layer of salt and sand coating the ground. The hairs on her arms stood up, and she sucked in a breath.

"You found the village." Viktor's voice echoed through the ruins.

Ophelia jumped and darted inside a cottage that was missing its entire back wall.

"This really has been a delightful All Hallow's Eve, Ophelia," Viktor called.

She blushed at the sound of her name in his mouth, then slapped both her cheeks. She replayed her mother's voice in her head: "Ophelia, it doesn't matter how cute they are. If they are trying to eat you, they're not boyfriend material." Ophelia sighed. Such a shame.

Viktor's footsteps grew closer. Ophelia mentally went through her list of spells that used salt, sand, blood, or all of the above. Well, spells other than *that* one. There were a few that would do for a quick diversion, but would they be enough to make it to sunrise? The sky was lightening by the moment.

"You've given me quite the chase, but I'm growing tired of playing with my food."

Ophelia quickly traced a rune in the sand at her feet. Viktor's footsteps sounded slightly more labored. The ground would be feeling quite boggy to him now. Ophelia kept her gaze on the horizon, willing the sun to peek over the ocean waves. Even a single ray would do.

Viktor suddenly appeared in the gaping hole at the back of the cottage. His expression was fierce. He yanked his feet across stones that looked smooth, but should have felt like quicksand to him. Any hint of playfulness or amusement she had seen earlier was gone.

Ophelia was breathless, but not from fear. Viktor Andrei looked like the most beautiful fallen angel she had ever seen. His dark hair was disheveled, flopping onto his forehead. His deep golden eyes were piercing, and his silhouette lit from behind by the rising sun was truly spectacular.

Wait.

The sun was rising. Ophelia felt the first rays warm her face. And there Viktor Andrei stood, most definitely still a smoking hot vampire and not a smoking hot pile of ashes. How very unfortunate. This time, Ophelia was breathless from fear. And a little bit because he was so beautiful. But mostly fear.

Seeing her expression, Viktor smiled, dark and victorious. "There really was a magical hare here, little rabbit. But I found and drained that creature many Hallows ago. Not only was it–" He brought his fingers to his lips in a chef's kiss. "–delicious, it also gave me this convenient ability to hunt in the sun and a truly insatiable hunger for magical blood. So, while this has been fun, our little game is over now. I will miss you ogling me in the office, but it shouldn't be terribly difficult to find your replacement."

Viktor crouched, his muscles coiled and ready to strike. There was nowhere to run. Ophelia briefly considered whether having

Viktor Andrei's lips on her neck for a moment was worth the horrible and painful death that would come immediately after. No, probably not.

Now Ophelia was embarrassed. Viktor thought she was a silly little girl, a dime-a-dozen admirer. For the past few months, she supposed she had been exactly that. Viktor had turned her into a simpering puddle. After her legacy of truly spectacular All Hallow's Eve projects, to be the subject and victim of such a mediocre project was humiliating.

As Viktor sprang forward, Ophelia clenched her fists and time seemed to slow. This was not who she was. She was Ophelia Dreadwood, three-time winner of Most Horrifying Hallow's Eve Project, voted Most Likely to Inadvertently End the World, and tamer of monsters. She breathed in the strength of the coven that had lived and died here hundreds of years ago.

Fly away home. Ophelia heard the whisper again, but this time the voice was excited, determined, not scared.

In one swift motion, she sliced her hand with a jagged cauldron piece, slapped her palm on the sandy ground, and spoke the word that wasn't a word. A gale blew up from the ground, lifting Ophelia's hair and throwing Viktor off balance. His momentum carried him forward into one of the stone walls, ramming it with his head and shoulder with a satisfying crack. Viktor groaned, but his voice was swept up with the sand and salt that swirled around the small cottage. He covered his eyes, but Ophelia needed no such protection.

She opened her mouth and let out a singing cry that rang above the maelstrom. A thunderous crash of water sent sea spray flying over Ophelia's grinning face. A massive creature flew out of the ocean, her green and blue scales shining iridescent in the new sunlight. Viktor lowered his arm to find the source of the crashing water, and his eyes widened in terror. Mariscaleth stretched her wings, throwing the cottage into shadow. She looked down at Ophelia with bright silver eyes, waiting. Ophelia looked down at Viktor, memorizing his beautiful face twisted into a look of shock and horror.

"Please," he gasped.

Ophelia turned back to Mariscaleth.

"Come and get it!"

The enormous wyvern swooped down and snatched Viktor Andrei up in her sharp diamond claws. The cottage walls collapsed under her giant opalescent blue wings as she took flight once again. She hovered in mid-air, a magnificent sight to behold, before diving back into the ocean depths.

Ophelia watched until the sea calmed. She sighed.

"Oh, dear," she said suddenly. She had forgotten to take the portal key from Viktor.

"Looks like I won't be flying away home any time soon, ladies," she called to the ruins. The ruins didn't whisper back this time. They let out a sigh of contentment instead. Nothing for it but to enjoy the beach for a while. She would figure out what to do soon enough.

Ophelia had only been sitting on the beach a few moments when she heard the telltale whoosh of a portal opening behind her. Jack and Annabell tumbled through the door, Annabell still in her sheet-ghost costume. Jack looked around wildly, holding up his hands as though he still had his werewolf paws and claws.

"Where is he?" he demanded.

Annabell tapped him gently on the shoulder with a bony hand.

"I think she already took care of him," she said with a smile.

"How did you know I was here?" Ophelia asked, standing and dusting the sand from her skirt.

"You left Viktor Andrei's papers on your desk. You, of all people, would never just leave papers unfiled before clocking out for the night. Also, did you even read his project? It was glaringly obvious he was going to try to kill you."

Ophelia shrugged. "I only got to the magic bunny part."

"So how'd you do it?" Jack asked, his shoulders relaxing fractionally.

"Mariscaleth," Ophelia answered simply.

"So much for a day off, huh?" Jack's smirk returned.

"I know," Ophelia sighed. "I'm going to have to make it up to her. I also think I'm going to need a tetanus shot." She held up her sliced hand. Bits of rust clung to the edges of the wound.

"Uh, yeah. You definitely need a tetanus shot," Jack said. "Let's head back."

"Aw, but I brought my candy," Anna whined. She pulled a bulging bag from under her sheet, the flesh of her arm hanging next to the bag. "Let's eat it here."

"Weird to bring candy to your friend's potential murder, Anna," Jack said, itching at the tuft of fur behind his ear again.

"I knew she wouldn't be dead," Annabell said with a giggle. "This is Ophelia Dreadwood we're talking about. Also, she just had the worst date of her life. She needs candy!"

Ophelia laughed, flopping onto the sand with her friends. "I don't think it was my worst date ever, but I would put it in the bottom three."

Myth Or Reality?

REBECCA M. ROBERTSON

F inding love on a reality TV show was not a decision Cecily
Taylor would have imagined for herself, nor one she made
lightly. She was a hermit, if you could call a billionaire who never
left her private island such a thing. Her sprawling villa had been
photographed by persistent paparazzi, but no one who earned a
rightful invitation had been allowed to publish photos, and the
internet was rabid for a glimpse.

The money came from a skincare line she conceived in her
kitchen from ingredients grown in her expansive garden—it had
blossomed into a global enterprise almost overnight. Her *Goddess* products were wildly popular with A-lister celebrities and
acne-riddled teenagers alike who would change skincare routines
the moment she dropped a new video on social media with her
latest tips on exfoliating.

With her internet fame and immense wealth, finding a man
who wasn't interested in her for superficial reasons had become

increasingly difficult. When the producers came to her a year ago, the idea intrigued her: a pool of thirty interesting, attractive men who couldn't be after her for her celebrity or money because they didn't know who they would be pursuing when they agreed to the show. After ruminating on the idea for months, Cecily had finally agreed, much to her sister's dismay.

Aside from believing that Cecily starring in a reality television show was bizarre and, frankly, egomaniacal, Dea worried that their family secret would be in jeopardy. Because beyond being a billionaire hermit and skincare guru, Cecily Taylor was also a witch.

"If I'd known you were this lonely, I would have used a love potion ages ago on some beautiful pool boy and saved us all the trouble," Dea said, fretting at her nails as Cecily added the finishing touches to her makeup in the elegant master bathroom. "Playing girl boss at your company and managing the island while you swoon your way across North America is not my idea of a good time, Cece."

The bathroom was cool white marble with golden sunburst accents; thick fur rugs and settees added warm creature comforts to the crisp, clean chamber—a harmony of opposites like Cecily herself. Cecily was a picture of delicate feminine beauty. Her long bronze hair fell past her shoulders in gleaming waves, her heart-shaped face and azure eyes made her appear innocent no matter how she behaved, and with a skincare line that nearly outsold Apple last year, her skin was radiant and supple. Yet Cecily was not a woman to be underestimated.

"Maybe managing the island isn't your cup of tea, but you can't tell me you didn't like standing in for me at *Goddess*," Cecily said, dabbing her lips with a light coral color from a small *Goddess* jar.

The carmine that provided the color was derived from crushed insects the way the ancient Egyptians did it. The old ways were the secret to all of Cecily's products.

"Fine. I liked it. I was overdue for a power trip." Dea tossed her raven hair over her shoulder. She was beautiful in her own right, but she wore disillusionment like a cape of thunderclouds. "I still think this is a monstrous mistake."

Cecily sighed. "Finding lovers isn't the problem, Dea. It's finding real love. Maybe this is a mistake, but at least I'm trying." At her feet, two large canines, more wolf than dog, huffed and resettled themselves, bored of sitting still for so long. When a large crew of visitors wasn't expected, Cecily spent hours roaming the hills around the villa, riding game trails across the island, swimming in the sea, and walking the beaches–ingredients were bounteous wherever she looked.

"I thought you'd sworn off men."

"No, you swore off men. I took a little break." Cecily wanted to shake her sister who was being purposefully obtuse about the whole situation. Cecily's previous forays into true love had been excruciatingly painful and epically disastrous. And then there had been the bitter rebounds and meaningless dalliances with a string of replaceable men until she'd soured on the whole gender and disabused herself of the very idea of love.

But time had worked its undeniable magic on Cecily. Time and her true nature. She was a creature of hope, as was anyone who found the source of their power in nature. Growth, rebirth, life, and, therefore, love were in her blood. "You know, it's true what they write about in all those books and love songs, Dea. Money, success, worldly influence—it's nothing without love."

"And I say love is a myth."

Cecily froze, her hand poised to set her face with finishing powder. "Really?" She quirked an eyebrow at her sister in the mirror.

Dea's stoney visage cracked as a self-satisfied smirk crept across her face.

"Fine. Then hole up in your rooms for the week, if you'd like," Cecily said, rising from her settee. Her white gown pooled to the floor like liquid granite. The wolf dogs got to their feet and padded to the doorway hopefully. "The Top Three and the crew are only allowed access to the east wing. You won't have to see a soul."

"Oh, I'll be around. Just because I disapprove, doesn't mean I'm going to miss this spectacle. Besides, you'll need me by the end."

Cecily settled her elegant shoulders back, a subtle indication that Dea had ruffled her feathers. "And who came to whose island asking for help the last time she had a male problem?"

Dea slouched against the wall in her black silk dress and sulked.

Cecily swallowed a smug smile. She didn't need to aggravate Dea further before the television people arrived. "I need to be at the dock to welcome them. Are you coming?"

"I certainly didn't wear this designer dress for you."

Cecily walked the bright halls of her villa, the open terraces bathed in rich sunset light, making her way down to the main dock with the dogs bounding merrily ahead of her and Dea gliding along behind her like a shadow. Cecily tried to ignore her sister's cynicism.

Dea had been weighed down with it ever since she'd returned to Cecily's isle. Besides, Dea's power ran through gems and stones, lava and deep earth—she couldn't help the darkness running in her personality like a vein of ore any more than Cecily could fight her optimism.

"Miss Taylor, sorry to interrupt," Cecily's assistant called, running to catch up to the sisters, her huarache sandals flapping loudly against the stone tiles.

Cecily paused to wait for Ximena. Her new assistant was a grad student from Guatemala who dressed in brightly-colored woven skirts like she had just walked out of the Mayan highlands, yet could navigate technology and the internet like a basement-dwelling hacker from Los Angeles. "What is it, Ximena?"

"Mr. Papadakis would like a brief word. He's brought his replacement for you to approve."

"Now?" Dea asked, throwing her slender arm toward the dock. "The TV people are nearly here."

Cecily calmly pushed her sister's arm down and smiled apologetically at Ximena. "Forgive my sister's manners—she doesn't have any. Of course I can take a moment for Mr. Papadakis." It was hard to remember a time without her gardener. He was one of the few men she allowed on the island, preferring to hire women as a general rule, and the only one she trusted. But his hands were as gnarled with arthritis as the ancient olive trees in the vineyard—she couldn't begrudge him his retirement.

"He won't leave the garden, says he doesn't want to spoil the television program," Ximena said, gesturing toward the profusion of greenery behind the villa.

"Time?" Cecily asked.

"6:03."

Cecily nodded and strode decisively across the terrace to the garden, Ximena on her heels and Dea following indifferently behind. The dogs noticed her change in course and raced each other to the garden in a burst of reckless speed.

If people thought her villa massive, the garden was its perfect match, sprawling across acres and into the hills beyond the residence, climbing through trellises and beds in a combination of loosely manicured surveillance and unrestrained wildness. Cecily would have preferred to tend to it all herself, gardening being not only a true joy for her but an integral piece of her craft, but it was simply too large. Mr. Papadakis had been a rare find, a man who spoke little, performed his tasks expertly, and never raised an eyebrow when he found her murmuring to the plants or harvesting under the light of a red moon. He was irreplaceable, as sentimental and emotional as that sounded.

Cecily held her white gown up as she entered the garden, knowing the rich, dark soil wouldn't muddy her dress if she didn't wish it to, but aware this fact would be odd to Ximena and whatever interloper Mr. Papadakis had brought to her island. Dea opted to wait by the gate. The old gardener was waiting beside the Cleopatra mandarin tree which was heavy with orange fruit. It could use thinning, but Mr. Papadakis had difficulty climbing the ladder now, so Cecily made a mental note to do it herself once the television people had gone. The air sang with its fresh, bright scent as if fruit had recently been plucked, but Cecily saw no evidence of it.

Mr. Papadakis stepped forward to meet her. "Miss Cecily," he began in his thickly accented English, "I bring my replacement,

Andreas. My grandson." He beckoned to the tree behind him. "Andre, *ela edo*."

The branches rustled as a man stepped out from behind the tree, his arms laden with clementines. "Your tree needed thinning," he said, nodding down at the fruit he carried.

"*Thrasys*," Mr. Papadakis grumbled, but his eyes twinkled. Cecily didn't speak Greek with Mr. Papadakis because she was rusty and embarrassed of her accent, but she understood it perfectly. Cheeky, he'd called his grandson.

"Yes, I know," Cecily replied, trying not to show her irritation at being told what she already knew about her own trees from a perfect stranger. She sized the man up. There was a clear family resemblance: a mess of curly brown hair, reddish-brown skin like the underbark of a cypress from long hours spent outside, and eyes the color of olives. He even had the beginnings of Mr. Papadakis's smile lines around his eyes, but she wasn't sure she enjoyed them as much on a younger man. He did seem cheeky.

"Andreas is my son's son. He knows much about the plants and the gardening. I teach him myself from the time he is very small. He is gone to university or else I bring him sooner." Mr. Papadakis looked like he might bust the buttons in his vest with pride in his grandson.

"And what did you study at university?" Cecily asked Andreas.

"Classics, mostly. My graduate studies focused on the literature of Ancient Greece."

"Ah, no wonder you need a job," Cecily teased.

Andreas took it in stride. "Follow your heart, they say. Study your passions, they say," he said, smiling sadly.

"Mr. Papdakis told you to follow your passions?" Cecily scoffed, trying to imagine quiet, solid Mr. Papadakis saying anything as romantic as that.

Andreas grinned. "No, Pappous told me not to bother with university, to stay and follow in his footsteps. I guess he has the last laugh after all, eh Pappous?"

"*Echo panta dikio*," Mr. Papadakis replied. *I'm always right.*

An alarm chirped behind Cecily, and Ximena consulted her tablet. "Harbor master says the boats will be here in five."

"Right." Cecily took Mr. Papadakis's hand and shook it warmly. "We'll surely be lost without you, Mr. Papadakis. Thank you for all your work and expertise. Your grandson has a lot to live up to." She looked Andreas squarely in the face as she said it, hoping he would understand she was serious.

Mr. Papadakis doffed his hat to her and gave a small bow. "It has been my great pleasure to enjoy this garden every day."

Cecily wished again that he were staying. He understood the beauty of growing things, the steadiness of the earth, the fierce struggle of life in a garden. She doubted the grandson with his head in the classics would appreciate her land in the same way. "Perhaps a trial period, if you don't mind, Mr. ...?" Cecily wasn't sure if Andreas was a Papadakis as well.

"Andre is fine," Andreas said. "And so is a trial period." He didn't seem bothered by her skepticism. He didn't seem bothered by much, so far.

Ximena's tablet chirped again. "Boats are in sight, Miss."

"I can't just write 'Andre' on your checks," Cecily said, annoyed that he wouldn't just give her his name and let her get on with her evening.

"Surely a woman who comes to garden in a silk evening gown with an intern keeping her schedule doesn't write her own checks," Andreas said with a twinkle in his eye.

Cecily's eyes widened at his impudence.

Mr. Papadakis cuffed Andreas with his cap. "*Skase!*"

"*Signomi,*" Andreas apologized to his grandfather, then answered Cecily with his name. "Andreas Papadakis."

"Nice to meet you, Andreas Papadakis." Cecily held her hand out to shake his, knowing full well his arms were full of fruit.

Andreas went to take her hand and the mandarins tumbled out of his grasp. He fumbled after them, but each and every one fell to the ground.

"Goodbye, Mr. Papadakis," Cecily said to her gardener.

The grandson looked up from the ground where he was gathering mandarins, as if she were talking to him. Cecily couldn't help the smug little smile that crept across her face at the sight of him crawling on the ground. It served him right after the way he talked to her. Andreas shook his head at her as if to say, touche.

Cecily waited on the beach alone as the sun sank slowly into the sea. Alone was inaccurate. The crew surrounded her at a distance, keeping out of the welcome shot. Cecily felt ridiculous at the staging. She'd already said hello to Grant, Mitch, and Paolo when they arrived at the perfectly functioning dock, but the director insisted they film the men arriving on the beach in individual rafts and coming through the last feet of water to her like heroes storming the shore at Troy. At times like these, when she was fully aware of how manipulated the show was, she regretted not listening to Dea. There was a reason she rarely left her island. A lot of reasons, actually, but this media circus she was now starring in was one of them. Hopefully, it would all be worth it. It had to be.

Cecily heard the whine of a boat engine coming from the east—from the dock—and saw Grant seated in the prow of the inflatable raft that appeared, his blond hair blowing in the wind. The boat pulled near to shore and Grant climbed out, not quite as gracefully as Achilles—but then again, who was—and splashed through the water to reach Cecily. Her heart beat faster as he came nearer, despite the cameras and the phony setting.

He took his sunglasses off, revealing unbelievable Paul Newman blue eyes. "This is some place you've got, Cecily."

"Thank you." Cecily never knew what to say in front of the cameras. They gave her lines she could try, but she sounded like a bad actor repeating them. There were times she could forget people were watching and be more like herself, but never during these intros.

Grant took her hands and kissed her on the cheek. When he pulled back, there was something knowing and mischievous in his smile, like they were sharing a good joke about the cameras. It was one of the reasons she liked him. He didn't seem to take the show too seriously, and he wasn't trying to perform like so many of them had, ones she'd eliminated quickly.

"I missed you," he said.

"It's only been a few days since Toronto." Cecily had visited the Top Four in their homes, eliminating Juan from Miami before inviting the Top Three to her island for the finale. Grant was a strategist for a leading company in Toronto, a thinker, someone who got things done. It was incredibly attractive.

"Still missed you." He squeezed her fingers, something he'd started to do when they were on display for the cameras but wanted to share a private moment with her. Something that was only theirs, that the cameras couldn't see.

"I missed you too." She stared into his blue eyes—she could drown in them if she weren't careful.

"And cut," the director called.

The tension instantly disappeared from Cecily's neck and shoulders. Grant laughed.

"What?" Cecily asked.

"You really do hate the cameras."

"I do," she said, laughing with him.

He kissed her on the lips then. Cecily leaned into him, relaxing into his smell, his warm body, his unhurried kiss.

"Every time!" The director said it like a curse. "I call cut and then you give me the good stuff."

"Don't worry, boss. I kept mine rolling," one of the cameramen called.

Cecily pulled back, her cheeks reddening.

"Don't mind them," Grant said, putting his sunglasses back on. "I'll see you soon."

After Grant had been escorted to his room and the scene reset (including footprints swept off the beach by a production assistant), Paolo's boat arrived. He was a director's dream. He vaulted off the boat gracefully, his white shirt mostly unbuttoned to reveal a physique like Ajax, and then he strode toward Cecily like he was in a Dolce & Gabbana perfume ad, dark eyes smoldering, his long hair unbound and wind-tossed. Frankly, Cecily knew they weren't a perfect match, but he was fun and so unbelievably sexy that she never quite wanted to get rid of him.

When Paolo reached her, he had no qualms about taking her in his arms and kissing her until she was dizzy. Cecily forgot the cameras, the production crew, and for a moment, her own name. When he pulled away, Cecily fought hard not to let her knees wobble.

"Welcome to the island," Cecily said breathlessly.

Paolo grinned. "It's paradise. The perfect setting for lovers." For some reason, the outrageous things Paolo said never came off as ridiculous as they would sound from someone else. His parents had immigrated to the United States from Italy when Paolo was a child, and it was clear he had an undiluted Italian romantic sensibility. He was a former firefighter turned model who had been scouted from his photo in a firefighter's charity calendar. When modeling was slow, he still picked up shifts at his old firehouse. Handsome and heroic.

The final contestant, Mitch Maloney, was actually someone that Cecily was acquainted with before the show. He was vice president of a makeup company that had been courting her business for the past year, hoping she would consider a merger. He had been a familiar face from several video calls with the company's upper management, but they hadn't spoken or even emailed individually. The producers must have been very pleased with themselves when they recruited him for the season. Cecily had been surprised to see him the first day of shooting, but Mitch had been dumbfounded when he first walked through the doors in his three thousand dollar suit and saw her.

There was none of that discomposure now. Mitch was smooth, polished, and confident as he came to her on the beach—even his relaxed island-wear was expensive and his cologne smelled like a private yacht on the Mediterranean. It wasn't his money that Cecily liked—she had enough of her own—it was that he wasn't intimidated by her success. Paolo never spoke of finances, but Grant became uncomfortable whenever the conversation strayed that direction. He liked to discuss business, but Mitch was the only one who didn't flinch at her power in the global economy or the fact that she owned her own island. There was something tantalizing about the way neither she nor Mitch could ever keep the upper hand when they were together.

"You look like a goddess, Cecily," Mitch said as he strolled up to her with his hands in his pockets.

"Do I?"

"Yes, a veritable Aphrodite or maybe a sea nymph to guide me in my quest."

"Your quest?" Cecily couldn't resist sparring with him. "Are you sure I'm not a siren? What would happen to your quest then?"

One corner of Mitch's mouth curved in a smile. "I suppose I'll have to throw myself upon your mercy." He took her hand and kissed it, his hazel eyes never leaving hers. Cecily had the sudden urge to run her fingers through his perfectly coiffed light brown hair and muss it all up, just to see how he'd respond. But she held back. There were cameras watching, after all.

She settled for wrapping her arms around his neck and embracing him, her fingers toying restrainedly with only the hair at the nape of his neck. She felt goosebumps rise on his skin, and he pulled her closer to him.

"Yes, more siren than savior," he whispered in her ear, his lips brushing against her deliciously.

You have no idea, Cecily wanted to say, but she restrained herself again. Whomever she chose would learn the truth about her craft, but the audience watching at home had no right to it.

Cecily's head was spinning by the time they wrapped filming on the beach. The crew took their equipment back to the dock on rafts where they would load everything up to the east wing. She took a private path with Dea that climbed from the beach to a terrace in the west wing. She felt giddy and silly and exposed all at once, her body still zinging from the touch of her suitors, and she was glad for the cool sea breeze that fanned her warm cheeks and rustled the vegetation clinging to the hillside.

"Well, that was sickening," Dea remarked after they had been climbing in silence for several minutes.

Cecily felt her heady excitement pop like a balloon. Leave it to Dea to lay waste to an evening with one snide comment. But Cecily was grateful to have her sister at her side through the finale, a bucket of cold water to throw in her face whenever she let the suitors' flattering words and intoxicating caresses go to her head like too much champagne. "Jealousy doesn't suit you, Dea."

Dea snorted. "Jealous? Of those affected celebrity-seeking oiled-up Ken dolls?"

"Don't tell me you don't want to take Paolo down to a private cove and–"

"Paolo is distractingly gorgeous as far as boy toys go," Dea conceded.

"I think he'd prefer the term 'Casanova'." Cecily shared a chuckle with Dea. "Honestly, you can have him. He's not going to make the final cut. I meant what I said before—I'm looking for love."

They paused when they reached the top step and gazed at the view: the sea nearly purple as the last hint of sun sank into the endless waters, stars glimmering overhead, and the lights of the villa twinkling like strings of fireflies across the island. The moon was rising behind them, but Cecily could feel it on her skin, the power of night magic alive in the air. Possibilities floating around, waiting to be snatched at and made into reality. Cecily felt hope rising in her chest. There was a man on this island that was her match in every way, she could swear it by the constellations overhead—Andromeda's elegant arms pointing down at one of them. If only she knew which one.

"Normally, I can't abide castoffs, but when you're through with Paolo, send him my way," Dea said languidly before slinking away to her rooms. Cecily shook her head after her sister—as ever, equal parts infuriating, amusing, and interesting.

It wasn't late yet. The kitchens were serving dinner to her guests in the east wing, but Cecily wasn't inclined to join them. As used to solitude as she was, the whirlwind of people invading her island unsettled and fatigued her. She considered returning to her suite and retiring for the night, shedding the glamorous silk gown, wiping her face free of her evening makeup, spreading her unpinned hair across a satin pillowcase.

Instead, Cecily retired to the garden. Her wolf dogs found her quickly, but they were too rambunctious from the presence of the visitors and she banished them from her side until they could calm their exuberance. She walked the meandering paths, pausing occasionally to smell sweet white jasmine or to whisper encouragement to the young almond trees growing in bashful rows beside the worldly pecans. She sat on a bench beside the trickling stream that began high in the hills and listened to the words it murmured, listened and sat long enough that the mountain lion who roamed the wild heights of the island ventured near and drank beside her, her tongue lapping quietly. The lioness observed Cecily with wise, amber eyes for minutes that lasted hours, or seconds, until she blinked slowly and padded away.

When Cecily rose from the bench, a dour thought with a voice like Dea's niggled that none of those men would be at home here. It was one thing for Cecily to play at belonging in society during the run of a TV show and another for a man to enter her world and embrace it. Cecily frowned, the notion distracting the rest of her nightly examination of the garden.

The villa was quiet when she stepped back onto the main terrace—even the east wing, where nearly twenty guests were housed. Dawn wasn't very far off. The walls of the east wing beckoned, singing their own siren song. Surely no one was awake to notice if she crept closer, if she traced her hand along the doorway and listened for misty fragments of their dreams. But when she approached the door, she stopped abruptly at the sight of the sapling in a large ceramic pot that stood like a sentry to the east wing. What was wrong with it?

Cecily tilted her head back and forth to examine every angle of the unusual plant. It was a flowering pomegranate tree, or it should have been. What grew from the pot was strangely contorted, like it was trying to grow in too many directions. It was obviously neglected—how long had it been since she'd ventured through the east wing? Were all the plants in such a state? But no, the jacaranda tree just across the path was neatly pruned and flowering beautifully. The bougainvillea that sprawled across the pergolas over the terrace were lush and vibrant. It was only this sad case that seemed to be suffering and half-wild.

Cecily sunk the fingers of one hand into the dark soil in the pot, feeling for answers. But the soil was fine—not too wet, not too dry, full of rich nutrients and pleasantly warm. She closed her eyes and listened, pressing her other hand against the bark of the little tree, but the pomegranate tree was silent. Even when she spoke magic words of truth and growth and clarity, the tree remained still.

"Hmm." Cecily wrinkled her brow at the stubborn little tree. It was very much alive, but it wouldn't listen to her and it refused to speak.

"What's that, Miss Taylor?"

Cecily whirled to find Andreas Papadakis on the terrace.

"What are you doing here?" Cecily demanded, her voice sharp from being startled.

Andreas looked puzzled. "I work here. Temporarily, at least," he added as he mockingly tipped his hat to her—one like his grandfather always wore, although Andreas's unruly curls looked like they might throw it off at any moment in a bid for freedom.

"Yes, I know. But what are you doing here now? It must be..." But Cecily had no clue what time it was or how long she had been ministering to the potted pomegranate.

"4:30 in the morning. Pappous likes to begin early on hot days."

It was going to be a hot day—Cecily could taste it on the air. She wasn't sure how Mr. Papadakis could always tell, unless he used something as mundane as the weather report.

"May I ask what you are doing here at this hour?" Andreas asked, raising one eyebrow at her, although his face was pleasant.

Cecily wanted to snipe at him that he certainly could not question her about her comings and goings in her own home, but she thought a better use of her irritation at the new gardener would be to set him on the case of the struggling pomegranate. He wouldn't succeed and she wouldn't feel guilty in terminating his temporary employment. "I noticed a pomegranate sapling that looks neglected. It's not like Mr. Papadakis to overlook a plant. Perhaps you could ask him why he did so with this one. Or better yet, you could revive it."

Andreas cocked his head to the side with curiosity. "May I have a look?"

Cecily stepped aside and gestured at the sapling. Andreas studied the little tree from each side, an intrigued smile playing about his lips the longer he looked. He felt the soil, as she had; he even touched the bark, as she had; and he went so far as to bring one of the leaves to his nose and lips, smelling it like he might ascertain its ripeness.

"She definitely doesn't need reviving," Andreas finally pronounced.

"She?" Cecily wasn't skeptical about certain plants having gender, it was the fact that he was so sure of it when Cecily couldn't get a read on the plant at all.

"Don't worry, Miss Taylor. I'll see to it. She's confused, is all it is. Before long, she'll find her course." He touched his fingers to his cap again. "If you'll excuse me, I need to help my pappous."

He trotted off into the gray morning light, calling behind him once. "Don't worry. I'll see to it."

"Hmm." Cecily stared after him until she heard noises from the east wing, and she hastened to her rooms for a few hours of rest.

Cecily woke with dark circles under her eyes and a foggy head, which wasn't a problem for someone with her talents since she knew remedies that made them disappear almost instantly, but she was glad her date with Paolo was first so she didn't have to be on her toes. It would be easy to slip into a lazy haze with Paolo in the scorching sun of the hot day Mr. Papadakis had predicted.

Ximena and the producers had planned three individual dates for Cecily over the course of the next few days: horseback riding with Mitch, an off-island adventure with Grant that Ximena was strangely excited about, and today's date, sailing with Paolo on the far side of the island.

Cecily had enjoyed teaching Paolo how to sail—what wasn't to like? Her arms wrapped around him as she showed him the ropes, his endearing excitement when he began to catch on, his hands rubbing her own *Goddess* sun protection cream across her back and lingering longer than necessary. It was undoubtedly cliche, but Cecily didn't mind. And now she was soaking up sun, dozing on the deck while the camera crew went ahead to set up equipment on the shore and Paolo did push-ups to "make his pecs really pop" for the cameras in the next installment of their date: cliff jumping. The only thing spoiling her peace was that wayward pomegranate tree she had discovered earlier. Why couldn't she understand what was wrong with it? Maybe the presence of so many guests on the island was throwing her powers off. The sooner the finale was over, the better.

A strong hand slid across Cecily's stomach, startling her into full wakefulness. She jumped at his touch, unprepared for Paolo's sensuality after what she'd been pondering.

"Sorry to wake you," Paolo said, wrapping his hand around her back and pulling her closer, "but the crew is gone. We have the boat to ourselves. It would be a shame to waste..."

Cecily pushed back against his chest. "Paolo, I told you. I don't want to have sex. It's too complicated with two other men that I care about as well."

"Come on, baby. I won't tell. The crew's not here to see." Paolo's fingers pulled on the strings of her bikini.

Cecily abruptly kneed him in the crotch. She stood swiftly while he was groaning on the deck. "If you touch me again without my permission, you *will* regret it."

Cecily rushed to the edge of the boat and dove into the ocean, eager to put distance between herself and the oversexed model. Perhaps Paolo wasn't as harmless as she'd thought. No doubt he'd take her physical rejection and flight into the ocean as encouragement to try harder. Some men were like that.

There was a time when Cecily was powerless to do anything about it. But Cecily wasn't powerless anymore.

That evening, Cecily found Dea changing for dinner in her suite, one she'd chosen for its wide, carved bed and the wall of glass doors that looked out over the turquoise waters. Dea caught one look at Cecily's face before holding up a finger in triumph. "You need my help! I told you you would."

Cecily sighed and sat on the edge of the bed. "I had to keep Paolo at bay with two hexes and an old-fashioned knee to the groin during our date this afternoon. I warned him explicitly, but he wouldn't leave me alone."

Dea pursed her lips with disappointment. "Why did it have to be the hot one? It's always the hot ones." She slumped on the bed next to Cecily. "I'm sorry, Cece. Are you all right?"

Cecily leaned her head against her sister's for a moment. "It brought back some uncomfortable memories." Cecily didn't like dwelling on times when she had been at the mercy of out-of-control men. It had been a long time, but the pain was still there like a puddle long after a storm. She tried to shrug it off. "He was never going to be my choice, anyway."

Dea put her slender arm around Cecily. "I'll help, Cece. I won't even say 'I told you so'."

"You already did."

Dea nodded. "That's right. I did."

The sisters laughed softly together until heavy tears began to roll down their faces. Dea understood, even if she couldn't refrain from gloating. She understood too well.

Cecily walked most of the night in her garden again, seeking the peace she found in moonlight and green things and her craft. When she returned to the villa at dawn, she wound her way to the east wing to check on the potted pomegranate tree, but Andreas was already there, tending to it with a bucket of water.

"Let me guess, your grandfather said it's going to be another hot day?" Cecily asked wryly.

Andreas didn't seem surprised by her presence. He smiled, the lines around his eyes crinkling pleasantly. "Pappous didn't say anything, though he'll probably have a lot to say to me when he realizes I came without him. He worries."

"Worries about what?" Cecily paced closer, observing the peculiar way he watered the tree in a spiral pattern. Spirals were symbols of growth, balance, and enlightenment. Interesting.

"He fears I annoy you." Andreas looked up at her from where he knelt by the pot, completely unabashed by his bold comment. Cecily felt heat rise in her cheeks. "I think he knows us both too well." Andreas chuckled.

Cheeky, indeed, Cecily thought. "When your grandfather showed up to work this early, he had the wisdom to keep to himself."

"I said I would see to her," Andreas said, his hand grazing the large pot. "Now is when she needed tending. And you see, she is looking better already."

Cecily did notice the pomegranate looked different, which most people would find impossible—trees didn't change their appearance overnight—but Cecily knew better. The trunk stood straighter, although the branches still stretched in odd directions, looking for sun in all the wrong places. "She doesn't know what's good for her," Cecily said, picking up Andreas's habit of personifying the tree without realizing it.

Andreas tsked at Cecily, a soft chide that somehow conveyed censure and camaraderie at once. "She knows."

Cecily nearly gaped at the man's affrontery. Where did he get the nerve to assume such familiarity?

Andreas seemed to feel her pause. "She knows," he insisted, beckoning her over. "Come. See."

Cecily hesitated, but made her way to the pot and knelt beside it. Andreas took her hand and placed it against the base of the tree. His hands were as rough as the bark, but warm and gentle. Cecily felt a tingling in her hand that crept up her arm, her neck, across her scalp—she had to steel herself not to shiver with the unexpected feeling. She grasped the cold pot with her other hand to steady herself. Was this Andreas or the tree waking up?

"You see, she's remembering already. Her trunk is reaching taller. Her roots are digging deeper." Andreas released her hand and pointed to the jacaranda and the bougainvillea. "I think these confused her, made her think she was just for decoration." He looked up at the little tree affectionately. "She is beautiful, but she has greater purpose than these prima donnas, yes?"

Cecily knew Andreas was asking rhetorically, but she had the urge to give him an answer, anything to keep him talking. She liked the way he spoke, not only the music of his voice, but the way he put things. "Thank you. I don't usually...I haven't been..." She sighed, unsure of what she meant to say. "I hired your grandfather because there is too much work for me to do alone, not because I don't know what I'm doing. And yet, this tree flounders right under my nose."

"You are clearly a busy woman, Miss Taylor." Andreas stood and offered her a hand up.

Cecily got to her feet on her own, irritated at his comment. "All this...to-do...It's only temporary. Television, fame—those things aren't important. They're not who I am."

"Is it really me you're trying to convince, Miss Taylor? Because I'm just your gardener. Temporary gardener," he amended. His eyes twinkled with a secret smile.

Cecily's wolf dogs trotted around the corner, summoned to the east wing, perhaps by Cecily's vexation. They circled her once, then wound around Andreas Papadakis, sniffing him to determine if he were predator or prey. Without a glance in her direction for approval, the dogs began nuzzling Andreas's fingers and rubbing their thick coats against his legs, hungry for his attention. Andreas scratched behind their ears and under their chins until their tails wagged like they were golden retrievers.

"I see you've met before," Cecily said, aware of the bite in her voice. What good were intimidating wolf dogs if they rolled over like lap dogs the first time a handsome face gave them attention?

"Yes, they've been following me around the garden. We're good friends."

Cecily had seen enough. She snapped her fingers and the dogs sprang to attention, dashing to her side. She needed to get ready for the morning and her date with Mitch. Why was she wasting time conversing with Andreas who thought she was a fame-seeking incompetent?

"Thank you, again," Cecily said in parting, already hurrying away into the pale morning light.

"Miss Taylor!" Andreas called.

When she didn't stop, he jogged after her. "Miss Taylor!"

Cecily stopped abruptly. "Stop shouting!" she whisper-yelled at him. "Are you trying to wake up the whole compound?"

Andreas lowered his voice. "I wanted to say—only the wise accept advice. Asking for help doesn't make you incapable. You are a most capable woman, Miss Taylor. I see that."

Cecily pressed her lips together and nodded, accepting the olive branch and returning with one of her own. "You can call me Cecily."

Cecily found Mitch at the corral, watching a great black stallion run in circles while the filming crew was busy setting up shots for their upcoming date. Cecily slid her arms around him from behind and murmured "Good morning" to his back. It was nice to stand still for a moment, enjoying the late morning sunshine and the birds chirping and the solid presence of the other without having to come up with a smart quip for the cameras.

"This fellow is quite impressive, isn't he?" Mitch said, when Cecily released him and joined him at the corral fence. The stallion was snorting and kicking his back legs, then running the length of the fence and rearing up on two legs, his forelegs pawing at the sky.

"Yes, he's a recent acquisition. Beautiful form, even if his behavior leaves something to be desired."

The stallion stomped to a stop in front of them and neighed furiously.

"Don't tell me you ride this beast," Mitch said with a laugh, taking a step away from the fence and the tall specimen of horse stamping in the dirt. "I know you're a fearless businesswoman, but be sensible, Cece."

Cecily stood her ground and stared the stallion down. "Not yet. He needs to be broken first. He's all testosterone and no self-control. A beast, as you say. But he'll come around. They always do."

As if he could understand her, the stallion quailed under Cecily's gaze and retreated to the far end of the paddock.

One of the producers waved Cecily and Mitch over. He was sweating profusely, even though the day was young and the real heat hadn't started yet. He fanned at his red face with a note which he passed to Cecily as soon as she was in reach. "Paolo ran off," the producer rambled, almost without breathing. "All he left was this note about how he wasn't ready for this serious of a relationship. Now the finale is ruined! And he won't receive compensation because he's in breach of contract. My dear Cecily, what you must be feeling! Is there any way you can continue with the filming schedule today, after such a shock?"

The note was short. It didn't take Cecily a moment to read. She flashed it to Mitch before handing it back to the producer. "I think Paolo and I both knew we weren't a perfect fit."

"Right. Then let's get you two into place!"

While the producer bustled away to pass along the good news that the shooting schedule wouldn't be delayed by womanly hysterics, Mitch scratched at the stubble on his cheek and smiled at Cecily. "And then there were two."

"You look entirely too pleased with the situation."

"I'm a numbers guy, what can I say? I like these odds better."

"Love's not about numbers, Mitch."

"I guess it's a good thing I excel in many subjects then," he countered.

"We'll see how you fare in the equestrian discipline." Cecily spun on her heel and walked up the path to the stables, feeling Mitch's eyes on her figure the whole way.

Mitch turned out to be an annoyingly proficient horseman. Cecily had hoped to dazzle him with her riding skills (which were impeccable thanks to her affinity with living creatures), but Mitch had gone to an expensive prep school where he was captain of the polo team. Cecily didn't realize polo was still played anywhere; she assumed it had gone the way of Latin, dead though the pretentious knew the rules.

They stopped for an over-the-top picnic that had been set up by the crew on a rise overlooking the villa. Tiers of desserts, platters of shining fruit, and a charcuterie spread took up an entire blanket, but that didn't matter for there were two more blankets piled with enough cushions and pillows to please a sultan.

Mitch propped himself up on a stack of pillows, but try as he might, he never got comfortable. It wasn't in his nature, relaxing on the ground. Even in a set up as glamorous as the one the production crew provided. Cecily tried to imagine him walking barefoot with her in the garden. She snickered at the thought. Ridiculous.

After the picnic, Mitch took her by the hand. "Let's walk for a moment."

"Alright." Cecily was surprised by his spontaneity. It wasn't like Mitch to do anything without a plan.

But as they walked down the path, the cameramen disappeared, and the director. And the production assistants. This wasn't spontaneous at all.

"Where is everyone?" Cecily asked.

"I thought we could use some real privacy. How can we have any kind of real conversation with the world potentially watching?"

"Did you pay them off to give us some space?"

Mitch tried to read her face. "Are you upset?"

Cecily shook her head and smiled. "No. I'm jealous I didn't think of it first."

Mitch laughed. "Of course, you wouldn't. You're too sweet." He put his arm around her as they continued along the dirt path.

"You have to have a killer instinct for these things. With your face and my business savvy, we'd be an unstoppable force, Cece."

Cecily stiffened under his arm, trying to absorb the way he insinuated her lack of business sense and labeled her as a harmless little thing in the same breath. She raised her eyebrow at him. "Are you talking about a relationship or a business partnership?"

"Both, ideally. Isn't that what's so great about us? We're a perfect fit any way you slice it."

Cecily stepped out of his arm and cut him off on the path. "Mitch, what are you talking about? Did you come on this show so you could get me to agree to the merger? Is that all this has been for you—some business strategy?"

"Of course not, Cece." Mitch reached for her hands, but Cecily pulled them out of his grasp. "Don't look at me like that. I didn't know who I was signing up for when I agreed to be on the program. But it was luck—fate, even—that it was you."

"Ah, yes. Your quest," Cecily said, feeling the picnic in her stomach souring. "Romancing me was a job perk. As long as you closed the deal, this was all a success."

Mitch ran a hand over his perfectly-coiffed hair, the slightest bit unsettled at the way this undocumented conversation was going. "Cecily, you're a businesswoman. Think about it from my perspective."

"Are you sure I'm not too sweet to understand what you're talking about?"

Mitch cleared his throat in frustration. "I was making an investment, an investment that has multiplied a thousandfold. I never expected to feel so much for you. I never dreamed I'd come this far or that we'd become this close, but I knew, regardless of the outcome of this show, I'd be returning to my company."

"And if you returned with the signed merger in your hand, you'd be a hero. Quest fulfilled." Cecily pushed past him up the trail, more disgusted with herself for falling for him than his ploy for her business.

Mitch grabbed her wrist. "Cece, that's stripping away everything else. We have a real connection. You can't ignore that."

"Yes, a business connection which I officially sever." Cecily yanked her wrist free, feeling suddenly claustrophobic. She had to get away from Mitch and the cameras and the crew poking their noses into her private affairs. Cecily veered off the path into the tangled brush, but she was immediately caught—Mitch had hold of her elbow now.

"Don't run away, Cecily. Stay here and talk this through with me." His voice was insistent, demanding, harsh. He was losing control of his deal. "We can come to an arrangement. We'll see eye to eye, I'm sure of it."

Cecily spun around and leveled him with her coldest stare. "Yes, before you leave my island, we'll see eye to eye. Make no mistake."

After Cecily escaped Mitch, she tore a wild path through the hills back to the villa, taking game paths when she found them and charging through undergrowth when she couldn't. Her clothes tore on brambles and her long hair snagged on branches until she looked like she'd been living outside for weeks, but she didn't care. As long as she made it back before the crew and Mitch. She had business to attend to.

Cecily blew into the villa like a tornado, scattering the lapwings wading in the fountains and startling Ximena at work on her laptop.

"Miss Taylor? What happened–"

"I need Dea. Now," Cecily said, not waiting for a reply.

Ximena's sandals flapped off at a panicked pace in the direction of Dea's rooms.

Cecily stalked toward the kitchen. As her staff had grown, Cecily had stopped performing her craft on the butcher block countertop and moved it into the airy outdoor kitchen on a private patio. The magic Cecily had in mind was best performed at night, but she could prepare the ingredients beforehand. They would keep.

Cecily nodded at the chef and her assistants when she invaded the kitchen, ignoring the dismayed glances they gave each other as she passed. So what if she looked like a survivor of a natural disaster? The staff had caught her in stranger circumstances before. It was one of the reasons they were paid so well.

When Cecily closed the doors on the kitchen and stepped onto her patio, she took a cleansing breath, relaxing a little for the first time since her flight down the mountain. She was safe here, from the men she'd so foolishly invited onto her island. The soothing scent of herbs, the peace found in meticulously compiling a spell—it would calm her racing heart and give her clarity.

A noise from the outdoor kitchen broke through Cecily's seclusion. Something shattering.

"Dea?"

Her sister wasn't at ease with her craft in a kitchen. She preferred open skies and starlight.

"Medea, is that you?" Cecily crossed the patio to her kitchen and pulled the glass doors open wide.

Grant stood in front of the cabinet that held Cecily's stained and faded grimoire, but he shut the door swiftly when Cecily walked in.

"Grant?"

Grant's ready smile flashed when he saw Cecily. "Looks like the date with Mitch didn't go so well."

When she stared at him in confusion, he pointed to her hair. "May I?" He plucked a leaf from the tangled mess.

Cecily swatted his hand away. "What are you doing in here, Grant?" She didn't have the patience to be wooed right now. She wanted answers.

Grant held his hands up and took a step back, giving her space. "I'm sorry. I know the crew is supposed to stay in the east wing, but I didn't think you'd mind if I went exploring. I want to share my life with you, Cece. I thought you wanted the same thing."

Cecily chewed on her lip. She wasn't thinking clearly after the incident with Mitch. She didn't want to take her anger out on Grant, but she didn't like finding him in her most private sanctum on the island. She'd rather have found him in her bathroom than her workroom. "It's been a rough morning," Cecily finally said. "If it had been another time, perhaps, but I really need you to go. I need some time to collect myself before we film again."

"Of course." Grant smiled at her wild hair again as he took her hands and squeezed her fingers—their secret touch. "I can't wait to hear about this morning."

Cecily released a reluctant smile. She stepped into his arms and let herself relax. Mitch had been a disappointment, a blow she hadn't seen coming, but Grant was here. Charming, handsome Grant, who wasn't trying to use her for her body or a business merger. She rested her head against his chest and banged her cheekbone into something in his pocket.

"Ouch." Cecily laughed at herself and pulled his phone out of his breast pocket. The screen showed the phone in camera mode. "That's interesting."

"What is?" Grant made a swipe for his phone, but Cecily dodged away.

She pressed the last photo icon at the bottom of the screen and a photo of her grimoire in its cabinet popped up. She paced around the kitchen, keeping two steps ahead of Grant as she swiped right and found four more pictures of the book. Detailed photos of her entire workroom. And the patio. And everything that lay between there and the east wing.

Grant caught up to her and nabbed his phone, but Cecily had seen enough. "What the hell is this, Grant? Are you a spy?"

Grant had the decency to look ashamed. "I'm sorry, Cece."

"Why?" Cecily's mind reeled. Grant, too? Was nobody trustworthy anymore? Was everyone in the world a two-faced pretender?

Grant hung his head. His Paul Newman eyes wouldn't meet hers. "I'm in debt. My company is folding. I can't afford my condo, my car, my lifestyle. Some online magazines approached me when they found out the finale was being filmed here. They offered a lot of money for the inside scoop on you and this place. And I had no idea who you would choose. I couldn't risk going home empty-handed."

Cecily's chest hurt. It felt heavy, like it was full of stones that banged and scraped against each other. If she were to jump in the sea, she'd surely sink straight to the bottom. "You could've talked to me. Why didn't you talk to me?"

Grant laughed bitterly. "Yes, Cecily Taylor in her ivory tower is going to understand my plight."

His words cut worse than his betrayal. "Is that really what you think of me?"

"I think being on the show with you has been a beautiful fantasy. But it's not the real world. You and I could never exist in the real world."

Dea appeared at the door in a loose black jumpsuit. All she needed was a pointed hat and Grant would really see something that supposedly didn't exist in the real world.

She took in Cecily's disheveled state and Grant's broken posture. No doubt she could smell the wreckage of their relationship in the air. "I did tell you." She looked pointedly at Cecily.

Cecily glowered at her sister. "Shut the door."

The producers couldn't believe their awful luck. All three finalists quit the show before Cecily could select a winner, before she even had her final date with Grant, the one Ximena had been so excited about. Mitch and Grant disappeared overnight like Paolo had, although Mitch sent a much more sophisticated email, stating he needed a break from the world to examine his priorities, and Grant admitted his scheme with the online magazines via text as his explanation for leaving.

When the entire crew loaded their boat the next day, the producers were still squabbling amongst themselves, one insisting the whole season had to be scrapped, while the others argued something could be salvaged.

"We'll be in touch, Miss Taylor, with our final decision."

Cecily waved to them from the dock, arm in arm with her sister.

"I thought they'd never leave," Dea said, watching the boat sail into the distance.

When Cecily didn't say anything, Dea scrutinized her sister's face. "You're still upset."

Cecily shook her head, brushing away a tear that had the audacity to trickle down her cheek. "This whole idea was stupid. Bizarre. Egomaniacal. Like you said. But there was a moment, when they first arrived...I could have sworn there was a match for me on the island. I heard it from the stars." Cecily scoffed at herself. "I can't even trust my own craft anymore."

Dea smirked. "Tell that to Mitch, Grant, and Paolo."

Cecily gave Dea a sidelong look. "You're enjoying this too much. As soon as they learn their lesson–"

"I know, I know. Back they'll go. But come on, admit it. It was kind of fun."

"It was gratifying," Cecily admitted.

Dea poked Cecily's side. "You know it was fun."

Cecily swatted Dea away and strolled up the dock toward the villa. "Alright. It was fun."

Dea was annoyingly chipper for the rest of the day. So much so that Cecily ultimately slipped away after dinner to check on the pomegranate tree in peace. It looked like a new tree. The trunk was tall and resolute, the branches stretched long and proud, and bright orange flowers were blooming contentedly, well on their way to producing fruit.

Cecily heard his footsteps behind her. She turned to Andreas. "Thank you for saving my tree."

"I didn't save her. Just reminded her who she was." Andreas shrugged like it was a small thing, only his duty as temporary gardener.

The wolf dogs started barking on the terrace, an excited commotion that couldn't have been caused by Ximena or any of the workers the dogs were used to on the island. Andreas cocked his head. "That doesn't sound right."

"No. I should go see–"

They hurried to the open terrace where the dogs were sniffing and carrying on about something behind one of the fountains. Cecily snapped her fingers and they ceased, trotting to her side obediently, but still filled with eager agitation.

Andreas circled the fountain first and whistled low and slow.

"What?" Cecily joined him.

Two gigantic pythons lay curled at the base of the fountain. One with skin so smooth and exotic that Cecily was reminded of a designer handbag, the other had arresting Paul Newman blue eyes.

"I know I haven't been around long, but I've never seen snakes like that on the island," Andreas said. He studied them appreciatively. They were beautiful specimens.

"They aren't native," Cecily agreed, watching the snakes twine around each other uncomfortably, unwilling to leave the shadow of the fountain and seemingly frightened of anyone coming too close. "Sometimes my sister and I rehabilitate wild animals. We recently acquired these two, and an oversexed stallion."

Andreas peered at her with a knowing look. "Pappous has noticed some of these cases over the years he has worked for you."

Cecily paused. She knew Mr. Papadakis had seen her at work in the garden, but she hadn't realized he had picked up on that aspect of her craft. "Really?"

Andreas nodded. "He worries for me."

Cecily searched his face, his olive eyes, the pleasant smile lines around them. "Do you worry?"

"Why should I worry? I am only your temporary gardener." Andreas teased her with his eyes.

"And what if I wanted you here on a more permanent basis?" She stepped toward him curiously.

Andreas took a step of his own. Cecily could smell the sunshine of him, the kiss of growing things on his hands.

"Then I would say that I take my craft quite seriously, too." Andreas took her hand, lifted it to his lips, and kissed a spiral of three kisses lightly into her palm.

Cecily's blood hummed with rebirth, hope, and the promise of good things growing.

Master of the Attic

INNA LYON

Wednesdays were Lydia's unlucky day—everything always went sideways. In the rental house on Turnpike Street, every day was Wednesday.

If Lydia Dreadknot, a skinny redhead in her early forties, were a real fortune-teller, she would've foreseen her future and not moved into that old house. She would've guessed that the monthly rent of $800 instead of the typical $1600 was too good to be true. But being an inexperienced witch and tenant, she failed.

Rather than trusting her instinct, she signed the contract, packed her stuff, grabbed her cat, and moved in. After dragging all seven plastic bins with her belongings into the house, she placed a handmade sign on the front door: Lydia Dreadknot, Fortune Teller. Open daily, 10-6, except Wednesday and Sunday.

The early October dusk settled in the corners of the old house while Lydia finished unpacking. Her cheap three-bedroom rental (pets allowed) came furnished.

"Muffin," Lydia called to her black cat, "have you seen my cell phone?"

Lydia often talked to her cat, though he never talked back. Muffin knew how to find things because his owner was so good at losing them. His name came from his uncanny ability to look like a chocolate muffin when he curled into a ball.

Rather than sniffing around for the phone, Muffin curled his back and hissed.

"That bad, huh?" asked Lydia.

Muffin pressed his ears to his head and stared into a dark corner, where an old-fashioned sofa with floral fabric stood. The cat grouped his lean body, ready to pounce on something.

"What is it? A mouse? Well, if you are not helping me unpack, then go check the attic for more mice."

Lydia could move objects a few feet with her mind and a wave of her hand. Placing the objects gently was a work in progress—she was still a witch in training. After unpacking, her front room looked like a beach after a storm, with her clothes, books, and fortune-teller trinkets in disarray. She would tidy it up later.

Exhausted as she was, Lydia dismissed Muffin's strange behavior.

"Meowyal!"

Lydia's cell phone glided across the floor from under the sofa. Muffin scrambled to the kitchen.

Lydia stumbled backward. The sound of stomping boots in the hallway made her jump and drop the stack of books she held in her hands. She stretched her arm and pulsed the energy in the direction from where she heard the noise. But nothing happened. There was no resistance or the sound of a fallen body—only tapping inside the walls and a distant door slam.

Lydia found Muffin shaking under the kitchen chair. She picked him up and gently patted him.

"I guess, the previous tenants left something besides the furniture. Let's check it out."

The spiritual world opens only to those who listen and believe. The stomping boots started a game without rules. If the unknown instigator of the sound didn't know the rules, Lydia did. Ghost or monster, he must answer three questions to the new owner. She grabbed her cell phone and marched to the end of the hallway to the attic entrance.

The house had no basement, but a vaulted roof meant there had to be a big attic. She tugged a cord near the light switch and pulled down the ladder. Considering the age of the house, the folded metal staircase looked like a Tesla dashboard inside a carriage.

"Let's go," Lydia called to Muffin, who plodded reluctantly behind her. "We are in this together. I didn't pay the animal deposit for nothing."

Muffin crawled up the stairs behind Lydia, ears still pressed backward. She expected a dusty attic with useless junk and the overpowering scent of mouse droppings. Instead, she found a neatly organized storage space with a few trunks and boxes in one corner and a red velvet armchair in another. The smell of pine-scented floor polish greeted her.

Lydia rubbed her forehead. Spirits and ghosts didn't wash the floor; it must be some flesh-and-blood being. Supernatural or not, Lydia wouldn't give up her awesome deal.

"Creature of the house, show yourself to me," Lydia ordered.

Silence.

"If you are bound by previous ownership, I free you as the new house owner. Leave this place and be at peace."

No response.

Should she report this anomaly to the coven? Lydia's mother had served as coven secretary for years, and she would know what to do.

"I demand you answer three questions: who are you, where do you come from, and why are you still here?"

Whatever this was, completely disregarding the rules of magic was definitely an anomaly. Pulling energy from the air, Lydia moved the armchair closer to her. She could manage only a couple of feet. A few uneven stitches of red thread on the hand rest showed someone had mended the fabric. Lydia had never learned to sew a button by hand. That's what magic was for.

Muffin took a few steps and jumped on the chair. He sat up straight and purred a few times.

"I wouldn't recommend staying here," said Lydia. "This place might have rabies."

Then she heard it—a sneaker. Lydia jerked, and Muffin closed his eyes. She went downstairs alone.

The stomping on the ceiling, the rattling of dirty dishes she'd left in the sink, books falling to the floor, and Lydia's blanket sliding off the bed lasted all night. She woke up with a headache.

Lydia called her mother in the morning to see if she could resolve the problem, but she didn't answer. Then she remembered Mom was away with the Department of Unexplainable Phenomena to consult on *The Witcher* movie. The first available appointment

was a week away. Lydia sighed and took the Monday evening opening.

Seven more days. She could deal with it herself until then. She
knew spells and magic for removing unwanted spirits. She didn't
know if they would work on the attic anomaly, but who said she
couldn't try?

But first, her day job. Two morning clients showed up
back-to-back.

A mother of three and her husband, with stage 4 pancreatic can-
cer, wanted to take their final trip together to Disneyland. Money
was short, and the mother debated if she should spend their last
savings on the trip or the treatment.

Lydia struggled with crystal ball visions. She managed a couple
of images and saw the client's husband's face with kind eyes and
a sad smile. The crowd behind him could've been anything from
park visitors to hospital staff.

Both tarot cards and coffee grounds foretold his upcoming
death and the mourning for the family. Lydia excused herself to
the bathroom and looked up her husband's page on Facebook. His
coworkers had created a GoFundMe account for the family's trip
to Disneyland. Lydia donated $15 to the fund and returned to the
living room.

"Please, put your right thumb into the coffee cup, touch the
grinds and swirl it right. Let's see if we can change the future."

Lydia's grandmother taught her that trick. The picture of the
swirled coffee grinds was always the same—rigid mountains that
the fortune-teller could interpret into anything. But if you placed
an idea into the client's mind that they could change the future,

they would do anything to follow the empty coffee cup predictions.

"You see," started Lydia.

She was interrupted by the sound of glass shattering in the kitchen. Both women jumped.

Lydia found her tongue first. "Sorry about that. My family can be so loud."

Muffin was her only family, and he always attended Lydia's sessions. But today, he wasn't there.

Lydia rushed to the kitchen. The garbage overflowed with bubble wrap, pieces of packing paper, and empty fast-food containers. A pile of used coffee cups sat on the counter, and the sink was full of dirty dishes. Everything looked normal except for the porcelain cups broken on the floor and the cat on top of the fridge.

"Did you do that?" hissed Lydia.

With a wave of her hand, she swept the pieces of the broken cup into the corner and returned to her client.

"Sorry about that. I was saying that by looking in your cup I see that something good will come along. Don't deny help and compassion from others. You are not alone in your grief. A Disney trip will be the best thing for your family."

The mother wept and said goodbye, leaving three five-dollar bills on the table.

The next client was suspicious that her husband was cheating on her with his business partner. She was polished but overweight, smoking one cigarette after another. She dismissed the coffee grind predictions and asked for a second round of tarot cards. Lydia also checked the crystal ball. The blurred image of a younger, more physically fit woman flooded the screen. Lydia had to break the bad news and tell her to leave him.

A heavy thud came from the ceiling every time the betrayed wife lit a cigarette.

"My husband is doing some repairs in the attic," said Lydia. She had to get rid of this noisemaker.

Amateur though she was, Lydia could still find ways to rid the house of negative energy. She didn't need a web search; she chose a spell she had learned in fifth grade.

"If I cannot kick that instigator out, maybe I can convince him to keep quiet."

She mixed dried lavender with a box of salt and brought the mixture to the attic with seven candles. Lydia sat in the velvet armchair to work her spell. It took her a minute to spread the salt mixture in a circle around the armchair on the clean attic floor. While she lit the candles, Muffin sat atop the soft padding. Lydia shooed him off. She needed to deal with the mysterious instigator, not get rid of the cat.

"Troubles, all gone.
Salt, wash away.
Spirit, leave this house
on the very next day."

Lydia was on her fifth chant out of seven when the doorbell rang. She pinched her lips together, trying not to swear, and went down.

A short, chubby woman in her sixties stood on the porch, holding a Tupperware with a red lid. "Hello there. Welcome to the neighborhood. I'm Mrs. Donna Cherybum, your neighbor. I brought you some cookies. May I come in?"

Lydia stepped aside, inviting the woman to enter.

After making herself comfortable on the sofa, Donna asked Lydia, "Are you a fortune teller? I saw the sign outside."

"Yes," Lydia nodded and added, "I volunteer at the animal shelter too."

"Oh, really? Me too. Which one do you volunteer at?"

"The one near my old place."

Donna nodded. "Family?"

"No, just me and my cat, Muffin."

Donna lowered her voice. "I've lived here for years, and this house has always been for rent. No permanent residents. The last family lived here for about a year. They took off suddenly and left most of their stuff behind."

"So, is this their furniture?"

"Oh, yes. They left overnight without packing and didn't even pay their electric bill. I assumed they were..." Donna looked around suspiciously.

"What?" asked Lydia.

"Russian mafia," said Donna in a mysterious whisper.

Lydia pursed her lips. The only furniture they'd left behind was a tube TV and IKEA bookshelves. She doubted Donna's statement about the Russian mafia.

"I don't think so," she said.

"You never know. You cannot trust every stranger on the block."

The women exchanged looks.

Donna continued, "What I was trying to tell you, that after they left, the house owner had a hard time renting out this place. None of the new tenants stayed longer than three days."

Three days? It was Lydia's second day, and she was already considering moving out.

"Have you noticed anything strange?" asked Donna.

"Not really," answered Lydia too quickly.

The sound of the vacuum cleaner from the ceiling above them broke the silence. Donna lifted a brow.

"iRobot," answered Lydia.

"In the attic?"

"Yes, I was thinking of sub-renting the space."

After the women exchanged cell phone numbers and Donna left, Lydia ran to the attic. The salty circle was gone. All seven candles sat in the shoe box. There was no vacuum cleaner in sight. Muffin was in the armchair, licking his paw.

"Did you do that?" Lydia asked, knowing it was a silly question. Even though Muffin didn't answer, her cat was magical to her. He gave her confidence during the fortune-telling sessions and helped her find lost things, and she hoped that one day, he would become truly magical and talk to her.

"Yes."

Lydia jumped. He did!

"No, he didn't. I did."

The deep baritone answering her didn't belong to the cat. It came from behind the armchair and probably belonged to the owner of the stomping boots.

"Who are you?" demanded Lydia.

"The keeper of the house."

"This is my house now. I order you to surrender and leave," said Lydia in a high-pitched voice. After a pause, she added, "By order of the Philadelphia magical coven."

A familiar snicker was all she heard.

Lydia remembered Donna's visit. "Are you with the Russian mafia?"

The creature mumbled something in a different language with hard rolls that sounded like swearing.

"Show yourself," continued Lydia. "Please, so we can talk."

"Clean your floor first. Then we can discuss further living arrangements."

Was he for real? Her floor? Wasn't she the one who paid for the house, including the attic? He was the peace-breaker and noise-maker. Did he just tell her that she was a bad housekeeper, too?

Lydia walked to the opening on the floor.

"Muffin, let's go," she called her cat. But Muffin was already curled up in the armchair, ignoring Lydia.

Lydia's knives, scissors, car keys, and a spare tarot deck went missing on Wednesday.

Thursday was divided between a sudden increase in clients and revenge on the attic's creature. Every spare minute she got, Lydia collected the candy, cookie wrappers, bubble wrap, and leftover food and went upstairs to dump it on the clean attic floor. Within the next hour, all the garbage had disappeared. No matter how sneaky and quiet Lydia tried to be, she never caught the owner of the deep voice and clunky boots cleaning the space.

Lydia noticed her house looked cleaner without all the garbage she brought upstairs. The kitchen table and sink were in order, too, since she needed clean cups for the coffee fortune telling and washed the dishes often.

Muffin attended all the sessions, but the cat sneaked into the attic when the last client was out the door. The red velvet armchair became his favorite spot for dozing and resting. Lydia wanted to believe Muffin liked the spot rather than the company.

She went upstairs, pretending she was searching for Muffin. A blue saucer with milk stood next to the armchair. She didn't remember owning that saucer. All her dishes were white Corelle, coffee cups included.

"Ah, that's where you went," Lydia called to the cat. "Are you drinking milk now?"

When Muffin predictably didn't answer, Lydia tried to start a conversation with the invisible tenant in the attic. "What is your name?" asked Lydia.

"Did you forget your trustworthy friend's name?" The hint of sarcasm in the deep voice bugged her.

"Of course, not. He is my cat," shrugged Lydia.

"Couldn't he be both? A cat and a friend, Lydia?"

"I guess." She pursed her lips. "You know my name. What's yours?"

"Not yet," replied the voice.

"What do you mean? I cleaned my house, didn't I?"

"You demanded three questions. I demand three biddings."

"You demand? Who do you think you are?"

"Yes. The house is not a home until it smells like good cooking and fresh baking."

"Me? Cooking and baking?" Lydia laughed. "Did you see that I don't own baking pans or even a mixer?"

"Well, no. All I saw was lots of fast-food containers and pizza delivery receipts."

Lydia felt her cheeks warming up. She forgot how much the contents of garbage could reveal about a person's habits.

"It is never too late to learn."

"When I'm older and have grandkids," Lydia snapped and turned to go down.

"You think I don't know how old you are?"

"Says the man who is afraid to show his face," she returned, grabbing the protesting Muffin from the armchair and marching downstairs.

Lydia huffed and puffed as she went down, realizing she had just called him a man. What if he were ugly, scary, and pure evil? The devil who's mending the furniture and washing the floor? She didn't think so and smiled to herself, imagining herself arguing with the invisible man over the scent of floor polish.

Lydia had eighteen clients between Friday and Saturday and had no time for shopping. She ordered Uber Eats twice and took the garbage outside herself.

Donna texted her that she would like to stop by to pick up her Tupperware, and Lydia replied, "Yes, please, do."

Donna came 15 minutes later with a Shih Tzu puppy on a short leash and a Walmart bag in hand.

"That's for you. A welcome present. You can open it later. Did you find a new shelter to volunteer at? There is one just a block away. That's where I go. Do you see this pooch? He is up for adoption, but the future owner wants to see if he will get along with cats. They have two. Call Muffin so we can introduce them."

Muffin was already coming from the hallway to see the visitors. The puppy squealed and pulled on the leash but didn't bark. Muffin sat in the middle of the hallway, observing the intruder.

"What a good doggy you are." Donna petted the puppy. Lydia bent to do the same. It took a few strokes between the dog's ears to calm him, but when she looked back, Muffin was gone.

Donna left a few minutes later with her Tupperware and the soon-to-be-adopted puppy. When Lydia opened the Walmart bag, she found a muffin pan with a box of liners. She shoved it away but remembered she needed to shop on Sunday.

When the universe conspires to bring your attention to something, it usually succeeds. When something is on your mind, you start seeing it everywhere you look. Lydia ended up at the cash register with four boxes of baking mixes and two jars of frosting. She bought milk, chicken, and potatoes from her list, but didn't remember writing any baking stuff. Oh, well, too late. The cashier had already scanned the frosting.

At home, Lydia poured the milk into a saucer and called Muffin. "Here, kitty. Come to the kitchen."

There was no movement or purring. She checked a couple of his favorite spaces. There was no cat. She knew where to go next.

"Have you seen Muffin?" asked Lydia, addressing the empty armchair.

Silence.

"Did you see my friend? My cat and my friend?"

"He left," a short reply in a somber voice came from behind the boxes in the corner.

"What are you talking about?" Lydia sensed the bitterness in her mouth. "Why?"

"You betrayed him."

"By doing what?"

"By petting another pet in his presence."

"This is silly. Are those dumb rules yours?"

"I don't tell him what to do. Muffin has his own mind. But we do chat about our problems."

"You chat? Then it is your fault he left. My cat would never obey the stupid rules of an invisible tenant." Lydia wanted to throw the boxes down on the head of that invisible voice. Instead, she plopped on the floor and put her hands over her eyes. What should she do?

"You have to find him and prove to him that you care," said the voice from the corner. "This would do."

A sheet of paper glided toward Lydia. On the page was a photo of Muffin in the red armchair, taken on her cell phone and probably printed with her printer. All she needed to do was add "Missing Cat" and her number. Muffin was a house cat, and Lydia hoped he'd survive the streets.

Why is it always raining when you are in a sour mood? Lydia thought. *Or maybe it is the other way around; a sour mood makes it rain.* Either way, it was a gloomy Monday evening. There were no phone calls about anyone seeing a black cat with golden eyes, even after Lydia had put up 85 copies of the missing cat announcement around the neighborhood.

The muffin baking pan from Donna sat on the counter, still with the twine bow and the package of cupcake liners. Four baking mixes were in the drawer, but Lydia had no desire to bake anything. She missed her cat, and baking would only exacerbate that loneliness.

When the doorbell rang, Lydia dashed to the door and threw it open, hoping for good news.

A tall, bony woman in a purple hat and black raincoat stood outside without an umbrella. Her outfit was dry despite the pouring rain, a skill Lydia had yet to perfect.

"Oh, it is only you, Mom." Lydia didn't hide the disappointment in her voice.

"Did you expect someone else?"

"Yes and no. Come in."

The women hugged, kissing on the cheek.

"I've heard about your missing Muffin. I'm so sorry. We don't feel complete without our cats."

Lydia put her mother's hat and coat on the sofa. She didn't have a coat hanger. Why bother to buy things if she would be moving away soon? The attic instigator could have this house. Lydia would have no fortune-teller business without her magic cat.

Her mother looked around, walked to the kitchen, and sat at the counter on the three-legged stool left by the previous tenants. "I see you have some new things—baking supplies, furniture that doesn't smell like your own. And no dirty dishes in sight."

Lydia whimpered once. "I don't think I will ever bake. That thing...that thing in the attic wants me to."

"Ah. The attic. That's why I'm here. The coven sent me."

"You?" Lydia blew her nose into the tissues. "But you don't work in the Department of Unexplainable Phenomena."

"Well, it has been a recent development. I'm now a researcher of unexplainable phenomena."

"Since when?"

Lydia's mother pulled a manila folder out of her tiny handbag. Lydia knew that trick—how to hide things in tiny spaces. The contents of her seven plastic bins filled all three bedrooms, the living room, and the kitchen.

"After your phone call, the coven sent an observer who visited you."

"An observer?"

"Yes, didn't you have a visitor that very day?"

"Well, only Donna. The neighbor with the Tupperware of cookies."

Her mother gave Lydia a dismissive look. "Really? Tupperware? I thought you were smarter than that."

"Well, I was paying more attention to the phenomena in the attic than a nosy neighbor with Tupperware."

"Tupperware," Lydia's mother explained, "that was the identifying device for rare creatures. To her credit, she tried to give you a hint about the Russian mafia and gave you a baking pan."

"She brought her dog with her," cried out Lydia. "And I petted the pooch, offending Muffin. Who knew he obeyed the rules of that, that..."

"Goblin. The Tupperware, I mean the device, identified him as a goblin. Well, a Russian goblin, anyway. They call them *domovoi*, meaning the keeper of the house. They come in their owners' shoes with a bunch of weird Russian customs. Goblins can be very obnoxious if you don't make peace with them. They don't like smoking, quarrels, messes, and other people's pets."

Lydia sighed. Everything made sense.

"What does he look like?" Lydia blushed.

Mother said nothing and pulled out the folder with a printed picture of a gray-bearded man in a brown knitted sweater. He had a wrinkled face, a bulbous nose, mischievous eyes, and a snickering smile. At least he didn't have horns.

Lydia stared at her crystal ball for a good ten minutes. From her previous practice, she had only succeeded in seeing a few images in the ball, making an estimated guess about the client's wants and needs. She was the client this time, and the first images didn't help. They were a blur of people's faces and didn't include Muffin.

"You need to concentrate on your inner feelings. The ball is a projector of your mind. Think about Muffin. Imagine where he could be. Care about him."

"Mom, maybe you try instead?"

"I can. But it is your cat and your magic. It's time for you to learn."

Lydia touched the ball with the tips of her fingers and stared at the shimmering glass. The faces of her recent clients swirled into a blurry blizzard of images. The mother who came on Monday was holding the twins' hands, wearing hats with Mickey Mouse ears. Wait. Did that mean the family made it to Disneyland? A quick picture of the betrayed wife signing divorce papers—good for her. A few other clients' requests and needs passed the ball and disappeared.

"Look for Muffin. Disregard everything else," commanded her mother.

Lydia exhaled and closed her eyes. Pictures of Muffin flooded her mind. She opened her eyes and projected those images into the ball with her mind.

Then she saw him: a wet Muffin in the back of a car, a golden collar left on the floor, hands pushing the cat into a cage, other cats, and dogs. A paper sign on a counter: "Thank you for your generous donations. Your money saves pets' lives."

"Mom," squealed Lydia, "I saw him. He is at the animal rescue place. But which one?"

"Good job," said her mother. "Get a bigger picture from above. Look for the street sign or a familiar location."

Lydia's phone chimed. It was a text message from Donna.

I saw a cat that looked like Muffin at the animal shelter where I volunteer. He got adopted today by a family with two little girls. Just checking if Muffin is OK?

"What?" asked Lydia's mother.

"All is lost," whimpered Lydia. "He is not there anymore. A family adopted him."

"Don't give up so easily. Search."

Lydia moved her fingers and tried closing and opening her eyes. More images of Muffin flooded the ball: Muffin silently screaming in the bathtub. Muffin dressed in doll clothes with trimmed whiskers. Two girls were trying to paint the cat's claws with red nail polish. One girl was crying, smearing blood over her cheek. A tall man was prodding Muffin under the couch with a broom.

Mother and daughter exchanged glances.

"The address," suggested the mother.

Fifteen minutes later, Mother's Suburban stopped at 4590 Greenhouse Street. Lydia rang the doorbell, and a tall man without a broom opened the door.

"May I help you?"

"I hope so," replied Lydia, opening a notepad. We are organizing a bakery fundraiser for our church's youth. Would you like to donate money or baked goods?"

"What?" asked the man, raising his brows.

"Baked goods. You know. Cookies, bundt cakes. Muffins!" Lydia yelled the last word into the house. A black shadow dashed through the door a second later and disappeared into the night.

"My cat!" yelled the man and ran after Muffin, pushing Lydia aside.

"I guess, I'll stop by later," Lydia said to his back as she returned to her mother's Suburban.

It took Lydia and her mother another twenty minutes of driving around the neighborhood before they found Muffin sitting under the swing on someone's porch. His yellow eyes glowed in the dark.

Lydia approached the porch and gently called, "Muffin, I'm sorry. Please, forgive me and come back home with me. I promise, my hand is not going to touch any other pets. No matter how cute they are."

Muffin came out slowly, like he was deciding if he could trust Lydia. He jumped on the ground from the porch, and Lydia picked him up.

She whispered into his wet ear, "We both miss you."

It turned out baking wasn't that hard if one knew how to read and had the muffin pan and liners handy.

While blueberry muffins were baking, Lydia made chicken and potato soup using her grandmother's recipe. The house now smelled like home. Hearty soup and freshly baked muffins. The other Muffin sat on the three-legged stool.

"Muffin, should we take some goodies to Donna?"

Muffin gave her a look.

"I think we could share the food with someone else," Lydia said, raising her eyes to the ceiling.

She placed a steaming muffin on a white saucer, and they went upstairs.

"Hello," she called softly. "I brought you some goodies. Will you show yourself?"

She put the saucer on the seat of the armchair. A shadow stepped out from the corner. The Tupperware scanning device didn't lie. Lydia saw the same face and nose as in her mother's folder picture—even the same brown sweater. But the eyes were different. They were kinder and bluer. He was shorter than she expected. Maybe three feet tall. And he was not a spirit but flesh and bone with those clunky boots.

"What was the third bidding?" Lydia asked.

"To share a cup of tea together," the man replied.

"Since your floor," Lydia accented the word, "doesn't have a table, maybe we can go to my kitchen?"

He nodded and stretched his hand. "I would like to introduce myself: Shishok, the keeper and protector of your home."

Lydia smiled and shook his outstretched head. Muffin rubbed against her leg. That's right, her home.

Legend Has It

WHITNEY OLIVER

I scramble up the hillside desperately, slipping down two inches for every five I gain. I grab at branches and leaves to help me move faster.

The late October air is chilly and a deep orange moon laughs at my efforts, half-hidden behind the storm clouds. It couldn't be a more idyllic Halloween, but I could be a touch biased tonight. I duck my head to hide my cheeks from the icy rain, and my dark hair whips in the wind.

Lightning flashes, illuminating the mud caked on almost every inch of my brand new mom jeans. Drat. I bought them two days ago, just for tonight. They were affordable, comfortable, and just stylish enough to make me look both good, and the appropriately 43-years-old that I am.

My date is three strides ahead of me, checking periodically to make sure I'm still keeping up. We were on the same page before we took off—we win at all costs, even if that means leaving me in the mud. I want to remind him. He's wasting time checking on me, but I haven't run this hard in years, and I don't have the lung capacity to utter a single word.

One of the other two couples is slowly falling behind. They're busy helping each other through the wild trees. Fools. I'm not sure what happened to the third couple. Carson and I will easily reach the broken-down house at the top of the hill first, as long as we can keep it up. It's thrilling he's as committed to winning as I am. I hate it when I'm the only eager one.

I push harder, trying to remember if my old high school gym teacher told me to breathe in my nose, out my mouth, or if it was the other way around. I feel like a teenager. Uninhibited, free, my heart bursting with an excitement I haven't felt since my twenties.

Carson is the newest science teacher at the high school where I also happen to teach health and history. We've been flirting in the faculty lounge since school started two months ago. I've made more coffee for myself at work in two months than I have my entire sixteen-year teaching career. He has a knack for bringing out the inner child in me, and I've been as giddy as our hormonal students since he asked me on this date two weeks ago.

I can't remember the last time I cared so little about being so muddy. Shoot, I can't remember the last time I was more muddy than a little splash on my boots.

Thunder shakes the trees around me. I jump, letting out an involuntary shriek of fear. Carson laughs, his green eyes bright in the moonlight. There's rain dripping from his beard and hat. His Minecraft flat cap is conveniently covering his bald head, making him seem ten years younger than me, so I'm grateful to see he's breathing hard too.

He glances at the couples now at least fifteen feet behind me, before stopping and holding out his hand for mine.

"Don't... stop..." I gasp for breath between each word, "...now."

His hand is warm, strong. His support steadies me in the mud, and I move quicker. Between breaths, he shouts over the pouring rain, "Number twenty-seven of tonight's 'Round Robin Trivia:' you clearly have a deep love for Elton John. Or Billy Joel. Is it Billy Joel?"

I pretend I can't hear him. He started his game of "Robin Trivia" earlier tonight when we were at the bar for actual trivia, keeping track of every detail he learned about me. No need to admit I don't feel strongly about Elton John or Billy Joel, or about seeing the cover band play their songs in three months. I am only desperately anxious to win the tickets because it means a scheduled date with him in three months.

Lightning flashes, illuminating a sagging rooftop with broken shingles just behind the patch of bare trees in front of us. "So close." I suck in a deep breath, wipe rain from my face, and let go of his hand to sprint with all I have to the house.

Carson keeps pace right behind me. A date in three months might be off the table after he's seen the out-of-shape, rain-soaked backside of me anyway.

Thunder clashes. I hold back my scream this time, but the ferocity of it makes me jump. And slip. I'm laying belly down in the mud and leaves when Carson hooks his arms underneath my armpits and hauls me up. That's not embarrassing at all.

He points to our co-worker, Emma, and her date. They found a pathway around the last bunch of trees and are about to take the lead.

I squeeze through the final gap in the trees, a few branches cracking as they get caught on my coat. Carson turns sideways and squeezes through after me, grabs my hand, and drags me sprinting toward the old house. We're still ahead.

Carson reaches out just as Emma's shoe comes flying from behind and hits the door a split second before his hand.

All four of us are half laughing, half wheezing. Carson plops down on the porch, laying down right next to the door, his arms and legs splayed. I want to lay next to him, but I heed the warnings of my best friend about my tendency to act too eager, too quickly and lean against a pillar instead.

I'm grateful for the overhanging roof. It might be sagging and about to fall down, but at least the rain is only dripping on me through the cracks instead of stinging my face. None of us speaks for at least five minutes while we catch our breath.

Then Emma sits down right next to Carson. I hate these games. If he responds positively to her eagerness, I quit. I just plain quit.

Emma is at least ten years younger than me, probably more. She accepted her first teaching job in the science department a few years ago. I have never been particularly close to her at work, but here she is on a double date with us.

Honestly, I want to not-so-gently remind her there are plenty of nice single men her own age. Us single ladies in our forties have enough trouble finding good candidates without young, tight-skinned, doe-eyed, twenty-somethings swooping in and taking them.

I've never met Emma's date, Noah, before. He's at least closer to her age, but he isn't doing me any favors, bent in half, his hand against the house, breathing the hardest of all four of us.

I'm dying to claim the victory, but this is our first date and I can't find the right words to show I'm interested in continuing to date him but still cool—not crazy, not pushy.

I suck at the dating game. Always have. Can't there just be an understanding that you communicate clearly, on a scale of one to ten, how interested you are and what exactly you're looking for in a relationship? No subtle hints. No guesswork. Just simple honesty, right from day one.

Carson speaks first. To Emma. "How in the bloody hell did you get your shoe off so fast?" I'm a little disappointed he's not as eager to claim the victory as I am, but I still force out a fake chuckle.

She holds her muddy wedge boot in the air like a trophy. "This old thing? It fell off about halfway up the hill."

Noah nods from where he's standing, chuckling hard enough that his slick coat makes swishy noises as he shakes. "I couldn't convince her to stop and put it back on." He shakes his head, still breathing a tad hard.

"Competitive much?" Carson asks.

"Speak for yourself. At least I didn't draw blood." She strokes the side of his face. No subtlety there. He turns to show me a scratch on his cheek next to his ear. Sure enough, blood mixed with rain is disappearing into his beard.

"Whipped by the final tree on my way to *our* victory." He stands up and lifts my hand in an awkward show of celebration.

I'm simultaneously pleased to have him so clearly walk away from Emma's touch and horrified to learn I whipped a tree at him without even knowing. I apologize and lift my other arm to get into the celebration. It all feels kind of awkward, but I hope it sends the right signal. The one that says thank-you-so-much-for-standing-up-when-that-young-hot-girl-touched-you. "Round Robin Trivia number thirty," I add to his game, "my competitive side is not attractive. Sorry about that."

He just laughs and wipes the blood with his hand. "'Tis but a flesh wound."

Light-hearted and fun, steady career, and awesome movie references. I'm ready to double down on his claim to victory and secure our date in three months, but Emma changes the subject, speaking directly to him. "I guess your friend and his wife decided the Elton John cover band tickets weren't worth it." She points down the hill.

He leans closer to me to squint down the hill. His beard smells like lemon and honey in the rain. Sure enough, headlights from the dirt road below flash through the trees as a car drives away.

I feel a little guilty we decided to race in the rain. I wonder if I would have been so willing if I were happily married for twelve years instead of on a first date, feeling giddy and eager to impress.

Emma stands up and even though she speaks to Carson, she at least goes to stand by Noah. "Didn't we choose the White Lady's house because she's the great-great-great-grandma or whatever of Martha?"

I feel bad I forgot the name of his friend's wife, and a little resentful Emma remembered it.

Carson shrugs his shoulders. "They won't care. They know what they're getting into when they come out with us non-married kids."

I force another chuckle at his use of the word kids, but my gut feels a little bruised. I wonder how many double dates he's been on with his married friends. Maybe his deliberate move away from

Emma isn't anything more than a sign of a practiced and polite dater. I've met plenty of those.

"So," I venture, keeping my voice as nonchalant as I can muster, "I think the bet was whoever touches the house first gets the tickets?" I emphasize the word "touches" as I look pointedly at Emma's shoe.

"Nobody said it had to be your hand that touches the haunted house first." Emma is ready, her defence locked and loaded.

There wasn't much of a chance for anyone to clarify rules. One minute we're getting soaked by rain in the parking lot, complaining about the bar giving us only two tickets for winning. The next minute, Emma grabs the tickets and makes the declaration that the first person to touch the White Lady's house gets to keep them.

A bet I'm sure was inspired by our earlier discussion of how fun it would be to go to the White Lady's house on Halloween after her tragic story was showcased in a trivia question.

She and Noah jumped into their car, and I got swept up in the challenge, running after Carson toward his car. "True, but I think it was implied that the winner would at least be the closest person to the house."

Emma doesn't back down. "You know what they say about assuming."

"Real mature." My voice is soaked with the annoyance I've felt about Emma all night, and I feel Carson distance himself a step away from me. Shoot. I shouldn't have taken a shot at her age. Too eager for the tickets. Too soon to show annoyance.

I'm trying to figure out how to salvage the situation when Noah pulls out his phone and turns on the flashlight under his chin. He wiggles the rusted doorknob theatrically. "We can't race up here on Halloween and be so eager to fight over tickets that we don't tell the story of the White Lady. That's just disrespectful."

His entire performance is effective, especially with the storm raging around us. He is clearly the kind of person who is good at defusing tension.

Keeping the light under his face, he swings the door open with a loud creak and grins boyishly, spreading his arm wide and gesturing us inside.

Everybody jumps right to it, walking past Noah into the house. I hesitate, a little unsure about trespassing into the house of the deceased, but I really don't want to leave on a sour note. I cross myself and silently say a prayer of respect for the White Lady before slowly stepping inside. Noah gives me a sideways look of confusion but just chuckles and follows me in.

The inside is damp, rain water leaking through cracks and broken windows. Any furniture that was left has either been stolen or is lying on the floor in pieces. What's left of the iron chandelier is scattered among the broken furniture. There's black mold growing in the corners and layers of graffiti cover the walls.

I'm horrified at the disrespect and say another silent prayer for the White Lady, apologizing. My desire to secure a date with Carson and my horror at the way we're treating the dead are warring with each other.

Noah has no such reservations. He pockets his phone and grabs two pieces of the broken furniture, theatrically using them as drumsticks along the wall. I cringe at how nonchalantly he touches her belongings.

The moonlight and lightning cast eerie shadows on Noah's face. One minute, I can only see half his face, the next it looks like it's covered in black scars that are only shadows from the tree, and then lightning flashes, illuminating it fully, making his eyes almost glow.

"Legend has it that long, long ago," he slows his drumroll, creating suspense, aided by the thunder outside. "A woman lived here." He speeds the drumroll again and I can't help but admire his commitment. The drumroll combined with the swishes from his slick coat create a compelling rhythm. I'm not sure if he's doing it out of respect, but it makes me feel a little better. At least he's honoring her story. "She lived here all by herself, back when there were only five houses within a twenty-mile radius of this town."

"I heard she never actually lived here. This house was built for her and the man she was supposed to marry." I can't help myself. That detail is pretty important to the story, and I want her to know I care about the details.

Noah glares at me with wide, comically shocked eyes until we all start to laugh. "Shh, Robin. So, as I was saying, before I was so rudely interrupted, rumor has it that a woman, betrothed to the love of her life—a handsome man, I believe I've heard. Kind of short. But stocky. Tough, ya know. The kind of guy who isn't classically handsome, but there's something about him. Brown hair. Brown eyes that are so deep you can get lost in them."

"Noah! Quit describing yourself." I'm glad Emma calls him out. I had surrendered my right to interruptions already.

"Just painting a picture of his rugged good looks is all."

"No arguments here. Please continue." Carson moves from across the room to stand next to me, the sleeves of our coats just touching. I was starting to feel a little chilled, but my heart starts racing again, warming me right up.

"As I was saying. Beautiful young woman. Handsome young man. All set to get married and move into their newly constructed house that will yield nothing but marital bliss." He gestures to the crumpling house around us and looks at me pointedly. I nod in appreciation before he continues.

"But the night before their wedding, the literal day before all her dreams, her deepest desires, you know, all that wishy-washy nonsense, was about to come true..."

Carson chuckles and I can't tell if he is laughing at Noah's delivery or the shot about marriage being desirable. I wonder if he still believes in marriage after his divorce.

"...disaster struck."

With the lightning flashing, the thunder rumbling, and the rain pouring down, I find myself completely drawn into his story-telling, even though I've heard the tale of the White Lady more times than I can count.

"Her most handsome prince was in a terrible," he draws out the word to a rhythm of despair, "accident. Trampled by his own horse while out chopping down trees. Lumber he planned on using to warm this very house on their wedding night."

"I thought a tree fell on him," Emma says.

I jump in next. The many variations to the story are my favorite part. "I heard he was mauled by a bear."

"Well, I heard he died choking on a peach pit." Carson already admitted at the bar that he had only heard references to the White Lady, and not her story.

His joke breaks the spell, and it takes another round of thunder and lightning, along with Noah beating his makeshift drumsticks to quiet our laughter.

"She searched the forest for hours, on a night similar to tonight. By the time she found his trampled, lifeless body, she was soaked to the bone, hair and eyes wild, her white wedding dress almost entirely brown with mud. A bride, deranged with grief."

I don't love the word deranged. Keeping it light to avoid any hint of the annoyance I displayed earlier, I step forward and spin in front of everybody, showcasing my wild hair and mud-stained clothes. "In case you wanted an image of how she looked. Minus the wedding dress," I acknowledge.

I hope the White Lady accepts my offering—a show that we are all grief-stricken from either looking for, trying to keep, or mourning the loss of love. I say another prayer, just in case. Overdoing it is better than underdoing it.

Carson smiles and grabs my hand mid spin, then twirls me again to pull me close, keeping his fingers interlaced with mine. I lean into him, basking in his warmth and my racing heartbeat, both barely keeping me warm now that the sweat on my skin is turning cold.

Noah drums to my spin and dives right back into his story. "The sight of her betrothed distressed her so much, she went insane."

That seems a bit harsh to me. I silently ask her forgiveness for the casual way he describes her pain.

"She became so insane, she never changed out of her wedding dress or uttered a single word again. She walked the town, wailing at anybody who got too close, eating discarded food out of garbages or right off the street."

Eating garbage? That's a bit extreme. "I thought she never left this house. She spent her days learning black magic and cursed all who dared trespass in what was to be her home of marital bliss."

"Or that." He continues, combining his garbage-eating lady with the one who practiced black magic, describing the miserable state of her looks and actions. I'm about to interrupt again when a person outside the window behind Noah distracts me.

It's a woman. Her hair is dark brown and wild, the wind whipping it around high cheekbones and a sharp chin as she runs through the trees. She's wearing a thin dress that I think used to be white.

I point, rushing past Noah to the window behind. "Did you guys see that?" I stick my head out, craning it to the left to see if I can still see her.

Everybody follows me to the window, but she's nowhere to be seen. "I thought I saw a woman. Nobody else saw her?" I don't say what I'm thinking, that the woman looked exactly like descriptions of the White Lady.

"Should we go search the trees for someone?" Carson asks, turning on his phone light and pointing it into the darkness.

I'm hesitant to make us all go back into the storm. "I don't think she was in distress or anything. Though she wasn't wearing a coat. She's got to be freezing."

If she can even feel the cold.

We stand at the window a few more minutes in silence, our eyes squinting into the rain. Noah eventually rolls with it, as if I had told him it was the White Lady in the forest or as if he planned the entire thing himself.

He begins the drumroll, this time on his knees, backing from the window toward the door we entered to give himself a stage in front of us again.

He speaks in a whisper, his voice thick with suspense. "Aren't we lucky? She decided to reveal herself to us this evening. Legend has it, she shows herself every Halloween, the anniversary of her lover's death."

"Only to those who are worthy," I whisper, crossing myself out of respect for her. Is my respect why I can see her? If I can see her.

Emma puts her own phone flashlight below her chin. "I heard she cast the house in dark magic to scare away trespassers, but on Halloween night, she comes back to personally scare them away. Stake her claim on her house."

A crash sounds from the floor above us. It sounds like something large was dropped or tipped over. My heart jumps. I try to convince myself Noah planned all this ahead of time. The woman in the forest. The crashing. But considering the impromptu race here, it's hard to figure out how he would have done it.

"So sad. How did she eventually die?" Carson asks.

"Nobody knows. They never found her body."

"I heard they found her lifeless body hanging from her dead husband's neckties, all strung together and tied to the chandelier." Emma sounds much too excited for somebody describing a suicide.

"I heard she was so grief-stricken she ran in front of a train to end her pain, bless her soul." Carson answers his own question. He has a way of making everybody around him laugh.

I'm dying to know what he believes about the state of the soul after death, considering he blessed her soul when talking about her. But I hold myself back, laughing with everybody else. That's definitely not a first date question.

Our laughter is cut short by another loud noise, this time closer. Something banging against the wall behind us.

Carson and I both jump at the same time, leaning closer into each other. I can feel slick sweat on my palm in his. I want to know who won the tickets and get out of here, but nobody seems to care about the tickets anymore.

I'll just have to risk being seen as too eager or forceful again. I'm too cold and nervous. "Hate to cut you off there, Noah, but it's getting cold, and I need to know how Carson and I are going to win those tickets."

I look at Carson to judge his reaction to claiming the tickets for us. He takes it in stride, nodding his head and squeezing me tight. My heart soars. Maybe we don't even have to win the tickets.

Emma mimicks Noah's drumroll with her palms on her wet jeans. She doesn't have his rhythm and the effect is not half as good, but I appreciate her keeping on the same topic. "Whoever finds the coolest artifact to keep from the house gets the tickets."

I'm horrified at the thought. "We can't disturb the things in the house. People have lived here. These are their belongings. Relics of their life." I cross myself for emphasis. "We can't take from the deceased."

How many times is too many to cross yourself on a first date?

Everybody laughs. Do they think I'm kidding? Before I can point out that I'm definitely not kidding, the woman from the forest walks in through the open door.

I jump so abruptly, I knock into Carson, forcing him to take a few steps sideways. His movement is subconscious; he's still listing alternative ideas to win the tickets as if nothing has changed.

The woman is looking right at me, smiling. Her hair is whipping around her face from the wind in the doorway. I look from her to Emma, to Noah, to Carson. If they can see her, they're doing a really good job of pretending she's not there. They're all still debating over the best way to win the tickets.

Her dark hair is knotted, wild and stringy. Her tiny feet bare and pale on the floorboards. But her eyes are bright, not haunted or distressed at all. If this is the White Lady, I have no doubt she's related to Martha. She looks frighteningly similar. Long thin face, high cheekbones, and blue eyes.

She walks through the middle of the room, stopping in front of Noah to mock him. She looks directly at me and rolls her eyes, her fingers clapping against her thumbs to mimic his talking. I can practically hear the words "blah, blah, blah," even though she's not making any sound as she moves her mouth.

"What do you think, Robin?"

Everybody is looking at me. I can't decide if this is an elaborate prank.

"Are you okay?" Carson asks, stepping a little farther away but keeping my hand in his.

The woman walks closer to Carson, looking him up and down with elevator eyes. She nods appreciatively and gives me a thumbs up. I'm shocked. Is this the woman who's supposed to be in distress?

All eyes are still on me.

"I'm fine. It's just..." My new friend blows me a kiss and runs out the door, knocking Carson's hat off with a swipe of her hand, revealing his bald head.

I stare in disbelief at the place she disappeared. Carson drops my hand to pick up his hat and follows my line of sight to the door. "Just what?" he asks, his voice a little quiet, unsure.

"Nothing. I think I must just be tired. I thought I saw something."

Carson doesn't take my hand again now that his hat is back on. I must seem crazy. Or maybe they can see the woman and they are all internally dying with laughter because I haven't just called them out.

"Did you guys plan this?" I make sure my voice is strong, confident. I look them all directly in the eyes, but they just stare back.

"Not really." Noah is talking slowly. "I mean you were in the parking lot when Emma dared us. I guess it just depends if you consider that a plan or not."

I don't know anybody in this room well enough to be able to tell if they're stringing me along.

It's silent for a moment too long. Emma breaks it, "What if the couple who stays the longest in the house gets the tickets?"

I'm still cold and dying for a warm place to curl up. How bad do I want this date with Carson?

Noah is all in. He's apparently excited to sleep in the abandoned house of a tortured woman. "Tomorrow's Sunday. I got no plans."

"No." Carson is quick to shut down the idea. "I can't stay the night." He's firm. No room for negotiation. I didn't really want to stay the night, but it still hurts how quickly Carson said no.

There's movement outside the door. It's a relief that everybody turns to look toward the noise. I wonder if it's the woman again. If it's her, she has more people with her this time. There's talking and laughter, and the sound of many footsteps on the porch.

"Do you think we'll get to meet the White Lady tonight?" Emma's voice is light, laughter in her tone, but I'm a little less certain. Anybody could be out that door. This isn't exactly the stomping ground of the innocent.

I back up, tripping over debris from the furniture. Carson helps me back to my feet just as a group of teenage boys walk through the open door.

"Miss Russo, is that you?"

I start at the sound of my name. I know that voice. That voice mocks me every other day in my third period health class.

"Hello, Jonah." I want to say something about him being in a place he shouldn't, but I can't bring myself to be a hypocrite, even though I know for a fact any plans I have are far more innocent than whatever he is up to this evening.

There are three other boys with Jonah, two I recognize, one I don't. The other three stand uncertainly in the doorway. I don't trust any of the boys I know, and I wonder if Emma and Carson recognize them.

This is not ideal on a first date. My teacher self is not my dating self, and honestly, I don't trust either of them to sustain a relationship.

Jonah is oozing his self confidence all over us. "Is that Mr. Miller and Miss Thompson. Is this a double date?" So Jonah knows Carson and Emma as well.

I avoid looking at Carson, who still has my hand in his after helping me up. I take a deep breath, using all the brain power I have to make myself sound like I am in control of the situation and not these boys. My desire to be professional wins over my desire to be a fun date. I hope it doesn't cost me Carson.

"Yes, and this is Mr. Smith." I don't actually know Noah's last name, but I'm hoping to elicit some respect from Jonah by setting us apart as the adults in the room. "These are some of our students from the high school, Mr. Smith." I look at Noah pointedly, hoping he doesn't contradict me about his name. "What are you boys up to this Halloween night?"

Jonah laughs cruelly and the other boys join in, not quite as confident. "Oh you know us, we're just out doing good. Cleaning up garbage. Helping the needy. That kind of thing." His eyes are malicious. I'm not surprised he doesn't back down. He is rarely under control in the classroom, where I do have authority.

"I hope so. You wouldn't want to be caught doing anything illegal or inappropriate out here."

His voice is sickly sweet. "No, we wouldn't want that."

Carson chimes in, friendly and casual. He's a natural with teenagers. "I take it you found those spray paint cans while you were cleaning up?"

Jonah just nods, a smile still on his face. "Just trying to keep our beautiful outdoors clean. We only have one Earth."

His friends are not as confident as Jonah. They fidget, clearly hiding cans behind their back.

"Here," Carson stretches out his free hand, "you've done enough good deeds for one day. I'll throw them out for you." I'm grateful Carson is adopting his teacher persona. At least we're on the same page.

Thunder crashes outside, making all of us jump. The tension is palpable.

"Now how would we feel any joy from all the good deed-doing if you finished the job for us? Don't you worry, we got this. Cute hat, by the way. My seven-year-old sister loves Minecraft too."

Carson lowers his hand. It's quiet, and I wonder if the other three adults are also trying to figure out the best way to excuse ourselves from this situation without knowingly allowing our students to participate in anything illegal. I can't see a way out.

Then, as if tensions aren't high enough, the strange woman is back.

She stands behind the teenagers at the door and blows air behind their ears. They must feel it because the first one shakes his head, the second moves farther into the room, and the third one swipes at his ears when she gets to him. Before they can turn to see where it came from, she hides outside the door.

Another clash of thunder sounds, and I can't help but think she somehow has control over it, even though I'm still not convinced it's not Martha and everybody is playing a prank on me.

She reappears and blows harder on the boys necks. They are visibly unnerved, unable to hold still, one cursing as they move away from the door.

She's grinning, enjoying every moment. She spins in circles like a ballerina, before slamming the door shut. The next thing I know, tin cans, sticks, and other types of debris are sailing in through the window.

Lightning flashes and Jonah's friends bail. They don't even call for him as they turn tail, throw open the door, and sprint into the downpour.

We look at Jonah, and he looks at each of us in turn. I can practically see his brain calculating his options behind narrow eyes.

The woman appears at the window and swoops both hands, the way a music conductor gestures the ending of a song.

Jonah is still weighing his options, and I feel better now that the adults outnumber him.He must come to the same conclusion, because he turns around, swagger and confidence still intact as he struts toward the door.

Just when I think we've avoided the worst, Jonah turns back around, a smirk on his face. "Remember, Miss Russo, you learn a lot about somebody when you tell them no."

I've watched Jonah flip condoms at the back of other kids' heads during the sex ed discussions for two years in a row, so I'm surprised he's able to spit out a quote from the lesson word-for-word.

"I'll keep that in mind." I want to scold Jonah, but I've been a teacher way too long to fall for his bait. He waits in the doorway, expectantly.

Thank goodness it's dark so nobody can see the flush I feel around my neck and ears. I avoid looking at Carson, just in case. Nothing like your student bringing up sex on the first date to make things awkward.

The woman is apparently affronted for me. Her jaw drops and she wags her finger at Jonah's insolence. Her anger is playful though, like she's also partly enjoying herself before she disappears again.

Pounding shakes the ceiling, causing dust to rain down on our damp skin.

"Were you meeting somebody here, kid?" Noah doesn't have the same practiced "teacher tone" as Carson. The slight fear in his voice doesn't help either.

"Maybe." I can't tell if he's bluffing to gain the advantage or if they really were meeting somebody here. "Why? Did we ruin the mood? Worried you're not getting any tonight?"

It's Noah who responds again. "Not cool, dude. You need to learn some respect."

Jonah smiles wickedly, he's getting exactly what he wanted.

Emma is nodding her head in agreement, staying close to Noah. The pounding continues upstairs.

"Respect for my elders?" I hate the way Jonah says the word elders, like it's a wilted brussel sprout somebody told him is good for him. "The same role models who I just happened to come across trespassing on private property?"

He has a point. And I'm not the only one who thinks so because we're quiet, the rain from outside mixing with the crashing from upstairs.

"That's a fair point," Carson finally says, "why don't we all leave the property together and head back toward our cars."

I think of the tickets for the first time since Jonah and his gang arrived. I don't think we're going to win them, seeing as Emma still has them tucked somewhere and Carson shot down the idea of staying here. Maybe it's best we were interrupted.

A deflated and bent bike tire flies in through the window, almost hitting Jonah. He gives us all one last look of contempt before strutting out the door. "You people are crazy. Can't believe you're supposed to be teachers."

My good mood is punctured. I'm not sure how Carson feels about a second date and I don't feel young acting like a twenty-year-old anymore. I feel immature and guilty.

Emma clearly feels no such guilt. The benefits of a not-fully-formed prefrontal cortex. She immediately starts praising Carson, sidling up next to him to tell him every impressive way he responded to Jonah.

She's not wrong, but she's pretty opinionated for someone who didn't say a word to any of the teenagers herself. Not to mention, she's technically closer to their age than she is to ours.

But as much as all of this is bothering me, I'm confused about the woman. How are Carson, Emma, and Noah not seeing her, yet not questioning it when objects fly from nowhere to chase the teenagers out of the house?

"Alright." I'm confident enough at this point to call them out. "Fess up. Who is she? And how are all of you so good at pretending you don't see her? Is this why you set up the whole story about how Martha is a descendent of the White Lady, bless her soul? That's good. You really planned this out. I'm impressed."

Emma cocks her head to the side and Carson stares at me. Noah just looks at his shoes.

"Gig is up, guys. I'm calling you out. Just tell me the truth."

They continue to stare. It bugs me. I like a good joke as much as the next person, but there's an appropriate time to be done. The time is now.

"Who is who, Robin?" Emma doesn't even seem sad to layer on the sarcasm and make me out to be a crazy person. I'm ready for "the White Lady" to start throwing things at Emma too. I'm ready for her to run off into the trees after Jonah.

They still just stare at me.

"What do you say we call it a night?" Noah is as done with this date as I am.

My heart sinks. I must seem utterly crazy. Running up here in the rain seems so silly now. What was I thinking? How did I think I wasn't being too eager?

Carson doesn't take my hand this time as we walk toward the door.

Nobody says anything about the tickets.

I want to curl up in a ball in the bottom of my shower, have a good cry, and just sit there until I'm warm all the way through. The plan already starts to make me feel better.

As I walk over the threshold of the house, I say one more silent prayer for the White Lady, crossing myself one last time, before putting on my hood and stepping into the pouring rain.

We walk in a line, slowly making our way through the mud and trees. Nobody seems to be in a rush or in good spirits. Noah is first, followed by Emma, then Carson, then me.

We're halfway down the hill when we see the flashing lights of Emma's car and hear an alarm going off.

"It's got to be those boys," Noah shouts as he lumbers after Emma, who took off at a run.

I'm also angry at the band of juveniles. They ruined the entire night. At the same time, I can't shake the feeling that the mysterious White Lady is still with me. I search the trees fruitlessly for her. She helped me all night. Why not now, getting rid of Emma?

And as if I summoned her, there she is, walking from the direction of our cars toward us. She waves at me, smiles, and winks, before climbing toward the direction of the old house. Her house?

"Do you really not see her?"

Carson looks at me out of the corner of his eye and smiles, just as lightning flashes in the dark sky behind him. "See who?"

"I can't tell if you're lying or not!" I want to force the truth out of him, but I have no leverage, no points by which I can convince him.

"So listen," he changes the subject entirely, "I'm terrible at the dating game. I thought things were going well tonight and now I'm not sure. It was a mistake trespassing in that home. I could tell you were uncomfortable with it before we went in. I'm sorry. And I know I'm rambling. It's a fault of mine, but can I ask you just one question? It's weird and it's backfired for me before, but I'm tired, I need to get home to my kids, and I'm too old to play games..."

A bubble of warm hope is growing deep in my gut. "Hallelujah," I say, "I'm so tired of games."

He smiles, taking my hand in his as we move through the trees. "On a scale of one to ten—and be honest, I can take it. I'd rather hear the truth than get strung along—how interested are you in pursuing this relationship as something serious? It would just help for me to know. I'm sorry I'm not better at this. And you don't need to answer now. In fact, maybe that might be better. Think about it and we can talk in a few days."

I want to silence him. I wanted to silence him two sentences in, when I could tell where he was going and hope rekindled somewhere deep under all my freezing layers. He took a risk in asking, so I take one, throwing my hesitancy to be too eager aside. "Ten."

We haven't quite reached the bottom of the hill, but he stops in his tracks and turns to look at me. Rain is dripping from the brim of his cap and his lips look as purple as mine feel, but his green eyes are bright again. "Ten? Wow, that was quick," his joking tone returns, "because I was going to say I'm about a six or so... so, that's embarrassing."

He slips his hand in mine to walk the last few feet down the hill. When we reach the dirt road, he turns, pulling me close. Rain still falls around us, our clothes sopping, but it's much warmer nestled beneath his jaw.

His voice is quiet when he speaks again. "All jokes aside, I haven't felt this way in a long time. If you're interested in pursuing this, I know I am."

I pull back to look at him, the pressure and insecurity of not knowing how he feels finally gone. "I spoke too quickly. I forgot to consider the fact that Jonah's seven-year-old sister also likes Minecraft, so you know..." I touch the tip of his hat and shrug my shoulders. "...you're down to at least a seven." I smile. "Sorry."

He smiles back, his eyes crinkling at the corners in my favorite way. He leans in, his eyes locked on mine. He's magnetic. I'm leaning closer without thinking. Then his eyes break contact and he's looking at my lips. My entire body is numb. But not from the cold. The sweet scent of lemon and honey reach me right before the kiss. His lips are slick with rain, but warmer than I expect. Soft. Inviting.

Bright lights break the spell when a car pulls onto the street, its windshield wipers dancing, horn honking.

We step back from each other and shield our eyes as the car pulls next to us. Carson's friend rolls down the window. "Get a room, you two."

Martha leans over him, holding out gas station coffee cups. "We weren't really up for a climb in the rain, so we thought we'd make better use of our time and bring everyone back some hot chocolate. What do you say?"

Her long, dark hair is wet and tangled. She's a mirror-image of the woman from the forest. I inch closer, peeking in the car as I take a hot chocolate from her, trying to see what she's wearing, but all I can see is her gigantic, calf-length puffer coat.

ABOUT THE AUTHOR

Amanda Siri Hill loves to explore inner demons through storytelling. You can find her short fiction on the Creepy Podcast, The Good Life Review, and Utah's Best Poetry and Prose 2023. Accolades include multiple First, Second, and Third Place awards at Storymaker's Conference and The Quills Conference. When not writing, she collects books and bikes in her South Jordan home that she shares with her husband and five children. Connect with her on Instagram @amandasirihill

To stay up to date with the author, join her mailing list at https://amandasirihill.com

ABOUT THE AUTHOR

Rae Wilkinson is on a lifelong quest to understand how the world works. She has pursued this quest through an early love of reading, a degree in mechanical engineering, traveling with her family, and through writing award-winning poetry, fiction, and non-fiction.

To stay up to date with the author, follow her substack

ABOUT THE AUTHOR

Rebecca M. Robertson writes clean young adult books with a touch of romance. She won first place for her YA novel, The Last Ingredient, in the 2024 Utah Original Writing Contest and numerous awards for her short fiction. She enjoys chocolate milk, overanalyzing movie plots, and exploring with her family.

To see more of her work, check out her <u>Amazon Page.</u>

ABOUT THE AUTHOR

Inna Valerie Lyon is a Russion bumpkin raised on a steady diet of cabbage and potatoes peppered with the required readings of Chekhov and Dostoevsky. During the day, Inna works as an accountant and at night, she writes stories about life, miracles, and cats. Inna is a member of the League of Utah Writers, the Infinite Monkeys, and currently serves as president of the Blue Quill chapter. She is an award-winning writer in different genres, writing in both English and Russian. She loves to see her readers laugh or cry...or at least, remember her story for the next fifteen minutes.

To stay up to date with the author, check out her blog.

ABOUT THE AUTHOR

Whitney Oliver loves collecting people. Mostly dead ones found in history books, genealogical records, or stories people tell of the past. She thinks people are pretty amazing (most of the time) and hopes to capture their passion, resilience, and the down-right relatable nature of their humanity in the fictional stories she writes.

Follow her work on her <u>substack.</u>